OTTO PENZLER PRESENTS
AMERICAN MYSTERY CLASSICS

EIGHT FACES
AT THREE

CRAIG RICE (1908–1957), born Georgiana Ann Randolph Craig, was an American author of mystery novels, short stories, and screenplays. In 1946, she became the first mystery writer to appear on the cover of *Time* magazine. Best known for her character John J. Malone, a rumpled Chicago lawyer, Rice's writing style was unique in its ability to mix gritty, hard-boiled writing with the entertainment of a screwball comedy. She also collaborated with mystery writer Stuart Palmer on screenplays and short stories, and ghost-wrote several titles published under the byline of actor George Sanders.

LISA LUTZ is the author of the *New York Times* bestselling and Alex Award–winning Spellman Files series, as well as the novels *How to Start a Fire*, *The Passenger*, and *The Swallows*. She lives and works in upstate New York.

EIGHT FACES AT THREE

CRAIG RICE

Introduction by
LISA LUTZ

AMERICAN MYSTERY CLASSICS

Penzler Publishers
New York

Published in 2021 by Penzler Publishers
58 Warren Street, New York, NY 10007
penzlerpublishers.com

Distributed by W. W. Norton

Cover image: Andy Ross
Cover design: Mauricio Diaz

Paperback ISBN 978-1-61316-219-4
Hardcover ISBN 978-1-61316-218-7

Library of Congress Control Number: 2021910052

Printed in the United States of America

9 8 7 6 5 4 3 2 1

INTRODUCTION

I'll start with the basics: Craig Rice was a woman, and her name wasn't exactly a nom de plume. Shortly after Georgiana Ann Randolph Craig was born, her artist parents absconded to Europe, leaving her in the care of her paternal aunt (or half-aunt). The aunt, whose married name was Rice, adopted her niece, tacking on yet another name. The future comedic crime author eventually boiled her moniker down to two of its shorter parts, a wise edit for book-signings.

All this happened a long time ago. Rice was born in 1908. Her first novel, *Eight Faces at Three*—this one—was published in 1939. She's been dead for more than sixty years. As I've wrangled with what my job is here, I keep coming back to one nagging question. With so many books to read—new ones, great ones, frankly more relevant ones—why spend your time on an author who's all but forgotten?

The thing is, she mattered once. In a big way. She still does, but I'll get to that.

Just seven years after writing this, her first novel, she was the first crime writer to grace the cover of *Time* magazine. It's impossible to understand how much that meant back then—there's just no modern equivalent. As always with fame, artistic achievement was only part of the appeal. Craig Rice lived a storied life even before she was published. One friend described her like this: "She was the only woman I ever met who could crochet, play chess, read a book and compose music at the same time—and hold a highball. I almost forgot that."

The word "bohemian" comes up quite a bit in the *Time* article. I suspect her three-to-four marriages (at the time of print) had something to do with that. For husband number one, I can find only the name and a description: dreamer. Husband number two was apparently a newspaper man. Somewhere in the mix was another marriage. She couldn't or wouldn't recall the name of her second husband in the *Time* article, although I suspect she could have picked him out of a lineup. Lawrence Lipton, the beat poet (and father of *Inside the Actors Studio's* James Lipton) was number three or four, depending on whether you count the guy whose name Rice couldn't recall.

In her prime, Rice was busy, to say the least. She wrote at least two books a year while also making her mark in the movies, cowriting two entries in the *Falcon* series, among other highlights. It was rumored that she ghostwrote for Gypsy Rose Lee. She didn't, but they were friends and even lived together for a stretch.

Rice was no stranger to ghostwriting, with non-credits including the actor George Sanders's debut novel *Crime on My Hands*. She published books under a few other pseudonyms, with and without partners. When *Who's Who* requested a photo of Michael Venning, one of her noms de plume, Rice posed in a fake beard, a hat, and one of Lipton's coats. If that doesn't sell you on her, you're hopeless.

It's easy to get lost in the fun, gossipy details of her life, but as you're going down that rabbit hole, it becomes clear that her last decade or so got pretty ugly. Like so many of her contemporary authors—and, I'd argue, any forward-thinking woman living in midcentury America—Rice had her demons. She tried to drown them in drink but, as the sad old joke goes, some of the bastards learned to swim. It's hard to write comedy when your world keeps getting less funny. Looking through the *New York Times* archives, I was surprised to find just as many notices of Rice's personal misfortunes as reviews of her books. She died at forty-nine.

I want to believe she found some laughs even during her darkest days. Near the end of Rice's career, she relied on ghostwriters of her own to meet deadlines. At one point she wrote to Lee Wright, her editor at Simon & Schuster, and asked whether she'd read her latest manuscript. "Yes," she replied. "Have you?"

I'd like to think that whatever state Rice was in, she still found that funny. Rice almost always wrote through the lens of humor. Those were the books she left behind, and that's how she should be remembered.

Which brings me to *Eight Faces at Three*, my own introduction to Craig Rice's work. Here's the spoiler-free premise: an old lady is murdered in her bedroom. Every clock in the house has stopped at 3:00 a.m. Her niece Holly finds the body and becomes the prime suspect. Jake Justus, press agent for Holly's bandleader fiancé (it makes more sense in the book), finds her at the crime scene.

I'll admit that for the first twenty or so pages, I was undecided.

Then Helene Brand walked into the room. Her looks are standard gorgeous, but she's wearing a fur coat, galoshes, and pajamas. The first words out of her mouth are: "What in hell goes on here? The place is crawling with cops and Nellie comes over with some insane story about Holly murdering Aunt Alex—God knows it was a good idea if she did." The sharp-tongued Brand sets the tone for the rest of the story. She supplies the booze, drunk-driving the plot forward to the very end. For her, the point of solving the crime isn't justice or getting a murderer off the streets. It's making sure the accused doesn't do the time.

While *Eight Faces* is certainly a crime novel, it's also a love story. Although we know it now as the first in the John J. Malone series, it reads more like the origin story for the Nick and Nora–style pairing of Helene Brand and Jake Justus. The book certainly owes a debt to the *Thin Man* movies, with gin-dripping banter stealing center stage from the crime in question. I'd never deny the charms of the William Powell/Myrna Loy pairing. I adore those films. But, ultimately, they're the Nick Charles show. I can't help but imagine what the Brand-Justus duo might have become if they'd been given more time on stage. They may share the detective work, but the spotlight shines most brightly on Helene in her signature pajamas and galoshes—definitely my next Halloween costume—skidding her Cadillac along the snowy Chicago roads.

Jake would be the practical one, reminding his wife of such boring concepts as sleep and speed limits. But I digress. As it turns out, John J. Malone, the gruff defense attorney, is the headliner of the series. This is Rice's first description: "He was an untidy man; the press of his suits usually suggested that he had been sleeping in them, probably on the floor of a taxicab." Malone is certainly a worthy hero—think Lou Grant with a law degree. And the good news, at least for me, is that Jake and Helene retain supporting roles throughout the series. Sometimes they help him solve the crimes, sometimes they're tangled up in the middle of them.

But the book you have before you is where it all begins. For Craig Rice, and probably John J. Malone, these were the good old days, when the champagne was still flowing and everyone was living like there was no tomorrow. I strongly recommend knocking back a few rounds with Helene and her pals. I promise you won't feel the hangover. More to the point, it's the only way we have left to hang out a while with Craig Rice.

—LISA LUTZ

CHAPTER 1

SHE WOKE slowly and unhappily. Her mouth was painfully dry, her head felt hot and swollen. There was a strange, faraway feeling in her stomach that threatened to materialize into a nearer, more positive and unpleasant, feeling.

What time could it be? She felt for the bed lamp, turned it on, blinked sleepily at the little onyx clock on the bed table.

Three o'clock.

She rubbed her eyes, sighed, yawned. Surely it must be later than three. She must have been sleeping for more than four or five hours. There had been a dream—

A dream—vague now, receding rapidly into unconsciousness and forgetfulness, but leaving behind an echo, an unpleasant echo. She struggled to bring the dream back to mind, to remember what it had been. Darkness. Something about darkness. And a rope.

A rope. Hanging. That was it. She had dreamed that she was being hanged. Only the rope had kept slipping and slipping. It had slid down over her shoulders and tightened over her arms. No, under her arms.

She stirred uncomfortably. Curious. Her underarms were

sore. Could a dream be as real as that? Impossible. But her flesh *was* sore.

She stretched, yawned, frowned, lit a cigarette and lay smoking it, staring at the ceiling. There had been more to the dream than the hanging. A dream of darkness, of standing in a cramped, dark place, an airless place, swathed in suffocating cloths. Like a coffin. No, not quite like a coffin. She had been standing up, not lying down. A coffin that was standing on end, perhaps.

She shuddered violently, shut her eyes. Silly and absurd to be so upset by a dream. It was all over now. She was awake, and the light was on.

Still, how to account for that sick throbbing in her head, the dryness in her mouth? She had felt perfectly well all day and at bedtime. An early bedtime. She had not had even one drink. The window—

She looked at the window. It was closed. Queer. She was sure that she had opened it before she went to bed. But it was closed now. Perhaps Nellie had come in and closed it. There was snow heaped against the window-pane, and it was bitterly cold outside.

She took a long drink of water, put out her cigarette and prepared to go back to sleep again.

But the clock.

She stared at it, blinked her eyes. The hands still pointed, crazily, to three o'clock. She picked it up and shook it.

Strange. The little onyx clock had never failed before. But now it had stopped, and refused to start again. Even if it did start, it would need to be reset. And she didn't know what time it was.

Damn.

She turned out the light, nestled down in her pillow.

It must be sometime after three. Might be any hour. She stared at the window. Was it getting light? The combination of winter darkness and new-fallen snow was deceptive. And the mornings were so dark anyway. It might be six or seven o'clock. Perhaps there was only another hour to sleep before Nellie brought in her breakfast tray.

Or perhaps it was only a little after three.

Then she remembered the other thing.

It had been a clock ringing that had wakened her. She remembered lying there, struggling between sleep and waking, hearing that persistent ringing, not very near. Probably from Glen's room. It had kept up for a while, and stopped. By the time she was wide awake it had stopped entirely.

But that was absurd. Glen had no alarm clock. Parkins always woke him. Even if he had an alarm clock, why would it be ringing in the middle of the night?

Or was it the middle of the night?

Imagination! she told herself furiously.

She turned her face from the window, resolved to forget the clock. She would think about something else. About Dick. The way he had smiled at her from the orchestra stand, as though he were playing for her alone. What a row Aunt Alex would kick up when she knew! Wonder what Dick was doing at this hour. Asleep in his room at the hotel? Or just leaving the orchestra stand after the last dancers had gone home?

What time could it be?

If she were to meet Dick in the morning, she must look her best. Meet him, and never, never come back to Aunt Alex's ugly old house again. In—how many hours now?

Surely it must be nearly morning—

What had that ringing been? Had it come from Glen's room? But *why?*

She must let Glen know somehow. Glen was her twin, all the family she had in the world, except Aunt Alex. An unlike twin, Parkins always said. But still, her twin. Perhaps she could get a word to him before breakfast if there was time. Time.

What time—

She swore softly to herself. If the clock was going, she probably wouldn't give two hoots in hell what time it was. Wouldn't even look at it. Now, when the clock was stopped, she was obsessed by the idea of time. There was no going back to sleep now until she knew what time it was.

And that ringing!

It must have come from Glen's room. But why? What was it? She had to know now.

Well, it was simple enough to find out.

She slid out of bed, shivering in the cold, hunted for her slippers, wrapped her bathrobe around her.

Senseless thing to do, go chasing around the house in the dark and the cold to find out what time it was. It didn't really matter. If it was morning, Nellie and her husband would be stirring around in the kitchen. But the house was as quiet as a grave. A grave. She thought again of her dream and shivered.

It wasn't only that she didn't know what time it was. It was that ringing, a ringing like an alarm clock.

The door of Glen's room was open. She felt gingerly for the light switch. Lights never woke Glen, he always slept like the dead. She pressed the switch, stood blinking for a moment in the light.

Glen was gone.

Glen wasn't in his room. His bed was empty. His bed hadn't been slept in.

Where could Glen be at an hour like this? Aunt Alex would raise the devil if she found out. Glen didn't have a key to the house. No, unless he had bribed Parkins to give him one, as she had.

She sat there worrying for a moment, forgetting her errand. At last she shrugged her shoulders, shook her head. It was none of her affair. Let Glen bury his own dead. Strange, though, for Glen to be out at an hour like this. She looked at his clock.

Three o'clock.

She didn't believe it.

Three o'clock.

She picked up the sturdy little leather clock, listened to it, shook it.

The clock had stopped.

Coincidence!

Funniest thing she had ever heard of! Both their clocks had stopped, and at the same hour. The same hour and the same minute. Talk about telepathy and such things! She rocked with sudden laughter.

Her laughter stopped short.

Where was Glen?

Glen was gone, his bed had not been slept in.

And both the clocks had stopped, at three.

A sudden panic swept over her. There was a shuddering echo of the strange dream, the dream of hanging and the coffin that stood on end.

And the clocks.

What time was it?

She had to know now!

There was the big clock that stood in the hall—

She ran into the hall, reaching for the light switch as she sped past it, on past her door, past the empty guest room, past the head of the stairs, to where the old clock stood half in darkness.

Three o'clock.

It wasn't possible, it wasn't true. The old clock in the hall had never stopped since it had been placed there, years before. It couldn't have stopped. It hadn't happened. It wasn't possible.

She stood for a moment, listening.

The dull, woodenish ticking of the old clock, deep-toned and steady, that she had known all her life—she listened for it while waves of hysteria rose to her throat and were choked back again.

Not a sound.

There wasn't a sound from the old clock. The old carved hands were still—the little hand on the three, the big hand on the twelve.

As panic flooded over her, she started to scream, stopped herself. Aunt Alex mustn't be wakened. Aunt Alex mustn't know that Glen was out. Aunt Alex mustn't know, mustn't ever know that she, Holly Inglehart, had been frightened into hysteria by the stopping of clocks.

And then again in the deathlike silence of the old house, she heard it again, distantly yet distinctly, that steady, relentless, persistent ringing.

Somewhere in the old house an alarm clock was ringing.

Nellie—It came from Nellie and Parkins' room.

She ran, as quietly as she could, up the narrow flight of stairs that led to the third floor, to the room Nellie and Parkins shared. As she ran, she turned on light after light, flooding the old house with a radiant blaze. There it was, the door to their room, there would be Nellie, and safety from the terrors that had followed her up the stairs.

And as she reached the door, the ringing stopped—

She knocked, waited, knocked again.

No one answered.

Nellie must be there. Nellie slept lightly. Nellie must answer—

She knocked again, louder.

Then she saw that the door was slightly ajar.

She pushed it open, slowly, hesitantly. A shaft of light from the hall fell across the empty bed, the smooth, neat, empty bed, the bed that had not been slept in.

Nellie was gone, Parkins was gone. The bed—

The clock—

There was a cheap alarm clock on the dresser, a painted clock with a strident, off-pitch ring and harsh, clamorous tick.

But it was not ticking now.

She knew what she would see even before she looked, the black painted hands pointing, the big hand to the twelve, the little hand to the three.

The cheap alarm clock stopped at three.

But it wasn't possible. She had heard it ringing, even while she stood outside the door.

She looked at it closely. The alarm was turned on, the alarm hand was set for six.

It hadn't been that clock she had heard ringing!

Forgetting her terror for the moment, she searched the room.

There was no other clock. Only the one that had stopped at three.

Yet in that instant the ringing began again, the same ring-
ing-remorseless, persistent, continual. But again it came from
the distance.

It came from Aunt Alex's room.

Aunt Alex would not be gone. Aunt Alex had not left her
room for fifteen years, not since paralysis had bound her to a
chair. Aunt Alex would know why an alarm clock would be
ringing in her room.

She raced down the narrow stairs, through the wide corridor, past the old clock, past the wide staircase, along the hall to
Aunt Alex's room, turning on light after light all along the way.

As she reached the door, the ringing stopped. But there was
another thing.

The door to Aunt Alex's room was wide open. Aunt Alex,
who should have been in bed hours ago (but what time *was* it?),
sat in her chair by the window, facing the door. She sat there
without moving, without speaking, her eyes glittering with
a strange, unearthly light as the lamp in the hall reflected on
them, glittering greenly, like a cat's eyes.

Holly stood in the doorway an instant, clinging to the door.
The old woman didn't move. Slowly the girl crept up to her.

The window was open, a freezing wind from the ice-covered
lake swept through the room.

Aunt Alex, sitting in front of that open window—

Forgetting her fear, the girl rushed to the old woman, felt of
her hand.

It was cold, terribly cold, and hard, like ice.

Aunt Alex hadn't known the window was open. Aunt Alex
was dead, dead and frozen as stiff as the icicles that hung over
the window.

There was something on the stiff pale silk that covered Aunt

Alex's withered old breast. Two gaping holes, not large, but terribly dark, and beside them what looked like a handle. She grasped it for one horrified moment, saw that it *was* a handle, the handle of a knife, protruding from the pale silk.

The room whirled around, she felt herself sinking into some unknown darkness, the darkness that had oppressed her in the dream. But as consciousness fled from her in a rushing stream, one last thing struck into her mind.

The clock.

The clock. Aunt Alex's little French clock in its little bell glass. The little wheel above the clock that had always whirled back and forth, all day long and all night long. It was not whirling now.

The fragile, gilded hands stood at three o'clock.

She saw it, marked it in her mind, caught at it with a last dissolving remnant of consciousness as she sank back into the welcoming darkness.

CHAPTER 2

THE FEBRUARY wind, blowing around the unprotected platform, was damp and raw. Jake Justus, pacing back and forth
on the snow-tracked boards, lifted his harassed mind from his
personal troubles long enough to reflect that he had never seen
quite so desolate a place. No, not in a lifetime spotted with desolate places. And this, he thought critically, in what was supposed to be a classy suburb, too.

He looked longingly toward the little enclosed waiting room.

The blond young man, Dick Dayton, pacing beside him,
nodded.

"Might as well go inside. I'd rather die from suffocation than
from the cold."

Jake stamped out a cigarette and the two men went into the
dingy waiting room. They were an odd contrast. Dayton was
slender, with a thinly handsome face, dressed immaculately in
what the well-dressed man would be wearing six months later.
There was a deepish wrinkle between his eyebrows, worn there
by twelve years of trouping across the country with third-rate,
second-rate, and finally first-rate dance bands. Now, his own
dance band. Dick Dayton and his Boys.

His companion was a tall, rangy man, big-boned and lean,

with an indolent slouch. Under an untidy thatch of red hair was an angular, friendly face with watchful eyes and a square jaw. There were wrinkles on his face, too; more than a few had been worn there by his job of press-agenting and managing Dick Dayton.

He looked disconsolately around the little waiting room. It was a forlorn room, smelling of damp wood, sweat, and cheap antiseptic. The benches were painted a dismal brown, the NO SMOKING sign was flyspecked and yellow.

"She's damned late," said Jake Justus, looking at his watch.

Dick nodded, looking out through the steamy window. A snow-packed road led away from the station; beyond it were brown, barren trees and the faint outlines of houses. A noisy little train halted abruptly at the station, disgorged a fat man in a green overcoat, a minister, and a pair of round-faced, giggling school-girls. Then it rattled away toward Chicago. Jake stared after it longingly.

"Of course," he said thoughtfully, "it's none of my business. But I'd say this was a hell of a day to be late."

Dick scowled deeply. "It isn't her fault. If she's late, it's because of something she can't help. That's what worries me."

Jake looked at his watch again, hoping he had made a mistake. He hadn't. It was ten o'clock. They had been waiting on the station platform since long before nine. He hated to think how long it had been since he had been out of bed before nine in the morning. Why couldn't people pick a reasonable hour to elope?

"Of course," he repeated, "you haven't told me all the details yet. But I say she's late, and I say the hell with it."

There was no answer.

"Well," said Jake Justus after a pause, "I only hope that she hasn't run out on you. After getting us out of bed before dawn. Besides," he added thoughtfully, "we'll miss the afternoon papers."

"Sure," Dick told him coldly. "This is just a publicity stunt to you. But it's something more to me."

Jake Justus grinned. "The dream of a lifetime come true, said Dick Dayton, America's idol, as he introduced his beautiful heiress bride to interviewers after a dramatic elopement—"

"Shut up," said Dick Dayton tersely.

"The headlines," said Jake soulfully, "will be something lovely—Angry Aunt pursues Dick and Bride."

"I'm going to get out of this place," Dick said sharply.

Jake followed him through the door. "Provided," he finished, "that she hasn't run out on you."

"She hasn't."

"All right, she hasn't. But where is she?"

The young orchestra leader frowned anxiously. "If she was going to get here at all, she'd be here now. She's nearly two hours late."

"Nearly, hell. She is."

"Something's happened to her, Jake. Something's gone wrong."

"I suppose Angry Aunt has locked her in her room on bread and water. Don't be a dope. This isn't 1880."

"You don't know her aunt," said Dick with feeling. "She *is* 1880. And she isn't normal. She might do anything."

"Are you trying to tell me that your girl's aunt is a screwball?"

"I am telling you," Dick said.

Jake shrugged his shoulders. "Well, I'm not going to take up permanent residence here waiting for her. This is the damnedest elopement I ever heard of."

"How was I to know she'd be late?"

"Are you sure you told her the right day?"

"Jake, something's happened to her."

"Are you sure you're in the right town?"

"Go to hell."

"These north-shore suburbs all look alike. I remember once I had a date with a girl in Wilmette. Her name was Clara—" Jake made an appreciative noise with his lips.

"You old Turk," said Dick admiringly.

Jake sighed. "I wish I had a drink."

The orchestra leader lit a cigarette, snapped the match into a pile of soiled snow, and strode suddenly toward the end of the platform. Jake swung his long legs after him.

"Come on, Jake. I'm going after her."

"On foot?"

"Do you see any horses?"

"Have they heard of taxis out here? Is this place too refined to have a main drag?"

Dick pointed ahead, past the row of weather-worn trees. Jake sighed deeply.

Just at that moment a taxicab appeared suddenly at the end of the street. They waved and whistled furiously. It slid across the pavement, turned halfway around, narrowly missed a tree, and shivered to a stop in front of them.

"Slippery today," the driver said. His face was pale.

They climbed in, banged the door.

"1216 Maple Drive."

The driver looked at them curiously. "You fellas lawyers?"

"No," Jake told him, "but I used to think—"

"Reporters, maybe?"

"Not now," Jake began, "but I used to—"

"If it's any of your business," Dick said furiously, "I'm an orchestra leader and this is my manager. Anything else you'd like to know?"

The driver grinned. "They don't want no orchestras at that address," he said cheerfully, and drove off.

Jake looked thoughtful. "I don't suppose you've thought of what you're going to say when you get there. Because if you haven't, I've an idea you're going to look awfully silly."

"I'm going to get Holly and get out of there."

"Just like that," Jake said.

"I've got a right to. I'm going to walk right in the door and ask for Holly, and if anybody tries to stop me—"

"Fighting again," Jake mused. "I wonder what the jail is like out here."

"There won't be any fighting."

"It would be easier," Jake told him reflectively, "to pretend you're the Realsilk Hosiery man, but this isn't my elopement and I won't give advice. Just the same, I don't like the setup."

"Why?"

"Well, your girl didn't show up, did she? And the cab driver seemed uncommonly familiar with the address. Of course," he added, "it may be nothing worse than a fire or an explosion—"

"Quit it."

They were driving down a desolate street, edged with leafless trees. Beyond the sidewalks stretched wide lawns, snow-buried gardens. The houses were large, most of them old and elaborate, all of them set far back from the road.

The cab took a corner sideways, skidded back and forth on the ice, missed a parked car by inches, and stopped in front of a pair of massive iron gate-posts.

"Here y'are," said the driver amiably. "Too bad you didn't

bring your orchestra with you." But Dick was already halfway across the sidewalk.

Jake gave the driver a handful of change. "And now, my garrulous Jehu," he began, "if you'll be so good as to tell us what's going on out here—"

The driver shook his head, grinning. "Go on in. You'll find out."

Jake muttered an objectionable word after the departing cab, shrugged his shoulders, and hurried after Dick.

A pair of great wrought-iron gates hung open. Beyond, a snow-covered drive, furrowed with the tracks of many cars, curved up to an immense and indescribably ugly house. It was a house of many angles, painted a dreary, mustardish brown, covered with porches, balconies, cupolas, little towers, and miscellaneous bits of ironwork. Jake wondered why anyone with money enough to own such a house would live in it.

"A wonderful spot for a murder," he told himself, "particularly the murder of the architect." With long, easy strides he caught up with Dick. "A lot of cars in the driveway."

"I don't like the looks of it," Dick said, his face grim.

"Possibly all the relatives in the world, come to look you over."

"Nobody knows about this, except you and Holly and me. Anyway, she hasn't any relatives. Just her aunt and—no, I don't like the looks of it."

"Want to go back and try it by telephone?"

"No."

"Maybe we should have kept that cab. We may get thrown out."

"We don't leave without Holly." Dick's face was pale in spite of the cold; the furrow between his eyes was deep.

"Dick, why don't you duck away and let me handle this? At least let me smell out the ground."

"*No!*" He rang the doorbell angrily.

After a long wait, a tall, thin woman opened the door and stared at them. Her sharp-featured face was pasty white, her black eyes seemed to look through them and beyond them.

"You can't come in," she said expressionlessly. "Go away."

It was not encouraging.

But Jake had his foot in the door.

"I want to see Miss Inglehart," Dick told the woman. "Miss Holly Inglehart."

The woman looked at them dully. "Go away."

"I'm sorry. But I must insist on seeing Miss Inglehart." Dick had a sudden flash of inspiration. "I've brought my lawyer with me and—"

He glared at her. A puzzled frown grew on her face.

"Perhaps you'd better come in," she said slowly. "Yes, you'd better come in."

She closed the door firmly after them, stood staring a moment.

"I'll call somebody," she said at last and went away, leaving them in the hall.

"Well, we're in, anyway," Jake said hopefully.

Dick shivered. The big, high-ceilinged hall was cold and dismal and dark. He tried to imagine Holly living in this house, living in it all her life, and could not. The brocaded walls were a deep, angry red, the heavily carved and ornamented woodwork was black. A stained-glass window in the stair landing cast greenish, yellowish, bluish blotches on the carpeting. A bearded man stared at them crossly from a large oil painting. There was an uncomfortable atmosphere in the place, sullen, unfriendly, and very cold.

A paneled door opened suddenly at the end of the hall; a red-faced, stocky man walked toward them, scowling.

"What do you want to see her about?"

Dick took a long breath. "I'm afraid that's my business."

"Not now it ain't," the man said peevishly. "Anyway, you can't see her."

Jake laid a restraining hand on Dick's arm. "Do you mind telling us if she's here, Mr. Fleck?"

A surprised mouth popped open in the red face. "Jake Justus, for Krissake! How do you newspaper fellas get places so quick?" There was reluctant admiration in his voice.

Dick did not seem surprised that the man knew Jake Justus. He was long past being surprised when anyone knew Jake Justus. "Look here," he began, "look here—"

Mr. Fleck shook his head soothingly. "You'll have to wait. Maybe we'll let you see her later."

"But why—" Dick began.

"Because she's under arrest," Mr. Fleck told him patiently.

"Arrest?"

"Arrest," repeated Mr. Fleck, even more patiently, as though he were speaking to an incredibly stupid child. "We're questioning her right now." He paused to scratch his nose vigorously. "Don't you guys know what's been going on out here?"

"We just got here," Jake reminded him.

"Well, the gal murdered the old lady last night and—"

A cry rose to Dick's lips—"Murdered!"

"Stabbed the old dame. Personally, I think she's a little ratty. Anyway, you can't see her yet."

Dick took a step forward. "You'll have to let me see her," he said desperately "I have every right to see her."

"Oh, you have, have you?" said the red-faced man mincingly. "And why do you think you can see her, pretty boy?"

Dick's face was gray. "Because," he said, "because she's my wife."

CHAPTER 3

"I'm NOT sure," said Jake Justus thoughtfully, "if you ought to have told him that."

They were waiting uncomfortably in the library of the ugly old house. The man named Fleck—Maple Park's chief of police, Jake had told Dick—had asked them a few sharp questions, learned that the marriage had taken place at Crown Point the day before and was to have been announced to the world today. He had learned also, with what had seemed like acute disappointment, that the young orchestra leader had spent most of the night before leading his band, and was consequently alibied by everyone who had danced that night at the Blue Casino. Then he had shaken his head dolefully and left them, after promising Dick that he would have a chance to see his bride before, he said dismally, they took her away.

Now they waited in the cold and dreary library. It was an impressive room, lined with unread books, paneled expensively in brownish-colored wood, filled with massive, dark, and uncomfortable furniture. Jake shut his eyes and wished he had a drink.

"No," he said again, "maybe you oughtn't to have told him that."

"Why not?" Dick asked. "We are married. And he was bound to find out sooner or later. Maybe she's told him already."

Jake nodded slowly. "You may be right at that. Still, it makes it look worse for her. What'd she want to bump off the old lady for, anyway?"

"She didn't do it," Dick said firmly.

Jake swore under his breath. He wondered what the girl was like. Dick's damn luck to get mixed up in something like this. The elopement had been the makings of a beautiful piece of publicity. But not now. "Band leader involved in murder of—" It wasn't a beautiful publicity story now.

He sighed deeply and wished for two drinks.

"Why can't they tell us something," Dick burst out suddenly.

"You'll read all about it in the newspapers," Jake said consolingly.

"Holly didn't do it," Dick said again.

Jake shook his head. "Maybe not. I don't know. I don't know anything about it."

The door opened and Mr. Fleck returned, mopping his face.

"She still sticks to the same story," he said wearily. "I tell you, she's ratty. Maybe she's working up an insanity defense. If she is, she's smart. So we'll take her down to the jail and—" he spoke like a man talking to himself.

Jake waved Dick away and prayed that he would keep his mouth shut.

"How did she do it, Mr. Fleck?" He could feel Dick glaring at him.

"Knife." Mr. Fleck mopped his brow again. "Funniest damn thing. Look. Last night—about eleven o'clock—Glen Inglehart—he's her brother—gets this telephone call from her—"

"Where was he?" Jake asked.

"Here."

"And wasn't she here?" Dick asked.

"How the hell," growled Mr. Fleck, "could she of phoned him if she had of been here? He gets this phone call from her, see, saying as how she's been hurt in an accident and she's at a hospital and she's been hurt but she ain't been hurt so bad but what she can be brought home, and for him and Parkins to come right after her."

"Who is Parkins?"

"'Ihere's a Mr. and Mrs.," the chief of police told him, "the servants here. Been here for years. So he gets Parkins and tells him about the accident, see. Now look. Mrs. Parkins, she's away, visiting her daughter. Daughter's name is Maybelle. Glen, see, he feels anxious about leaving the old lady alone, but he feels like they had both ought to go. Parkins, he thinks the old lady will be all right, on account of she's been left alone in the house before. Glen, he goes up and asks her what they had better do. Well, the old lady says sure, go ahead. So Glen, he tells Parkins to get the car out, and he gets his overcoat and they go to this hospital."

"What hospital?"

"The one where she told them she was at," said Mr. Fleck patiently. "St. Luke's. Clear down past the Loop. Only they stop on the way and get Mrs. Parkins, see, on account of maybe the girl isn't feeling so good, and it would be a help to have Mrs. Parkins along. So when they get to this hospital, what do they find?"

"Don't tell me," Jake said imploringly, "let me guess."

"They find she ain't there and she ain't never been there." He glared at them as though they might offer some explanation.

"Why didn't she call me?" Dick said suddenly. "If she'd been in an accident, why didn't she call *me?*"

"She hadn't been in no accident," Mr. Fleck told him, "she hadn't been in no accident of any kind, without you could call murdering your poor old aunt an accident, which of course it might of been if she was genuinely nuts when she done it."

Jake blinked a little. "What did her brother—and the Parkinses—do then?"

"Well, they wasted some time phoning the other hospitals in case there had been a mistake, which there hadn't. So then they came back here. Took some time, of course, with the roads being like they are. Bad roads. Like glass. And of course, being anxious about the old lady, on account of never leaving her alone under any circumstances unless it was absolutely necessary, which this was, as soon as they did get home, which was about four o'clock on account of the roads, Mrs. Parkins and Glen, they went right up to the old lady's room," he paused for breath, leaving them to cope with his sentence as best they could.

"Well?"

"She was dead," said Mr. Fleck triumphantly, as though he had produced a corpse out of his hat. "Dead and froze stiffer'n a board. Window was wide open and she was sitting right in front of it. Still is, if you want to look at her. She ain't been took away yet. And she was stabbed three times. Three, mind you. Once would have been enough, a weak old lady like her. What'd she want to go and stab the old dame three times for?"

"And Holly?" Dick asked desperately. "Where was she? What had happened to her?"

"She was right there in the old lady's room. That's where she was." He looked as though he expected them to contradict the statement. "Fainted dead away on the floor she was. Right where she'd fell after she stabbed the old lady."

"Couldn't someone," asked Jake, "have come in while everybody was away and done the murder? And when the girl discovered it, she fainted—"

Mr. Fleck shook his head vigorously. "No. Because there wasn't no reason for nobody else to have done it except the girl."

Jake's frown stopped Dick's interruption.

"And now," said Mr. Fleck aggrievedly, "now she tells some Goddamn crazy story about the clocks."

They looked at him, startled.

"Did you say clocks?" Jake asked blankly. He wondered if possibly Mr. Fleck, and not the girl, was crazy. Or else he himself.

"The clocks," Mr. Fleck repeated. "And the funny damn thing is that they all were stopped at three o'clock. All of them, mind you."

Mr. Fleck pointed. A little electric clock stood on the table. There was a mahogany clock on the greenish marble mantelpiece. Their motionless hands pointed to three o'clock. Jake repressed a sudden violent desire to look at his own watch.

"The whole thing is nuts," said Mr. Fleck unhappily. "She says—" he paused, gulped, and then told them Holly's story of wakening to find Glen and the Parkinses gone, their beds not slept in, and Alexandria Inglehart murdered at her open window.

When Fleck had finished, Jake looked sympathetically at the pale young man. "Tell me," he began, "did the girl ever act funny when she was with you? As if this was coming on? Just a bit on the screwball side?"

Dick shook his head. "Never. I can't believe it. There must be some explanation for this. Something."

"Sure," said Mr. Fleck reassuringly, "the girl's gone nuts."

A door opened suddenly; at once the room seemed to be filled with people. Jake recognized Hyme Mendel from the district attorney's office, a little man with a gold pince-nez—that would be Hedberg the coroner, Andy Ahearn from the sheriff's office, and a half dozen others who were strangers to him. One, he decided, must be Glen Inglehart, twin brother of the girl held for murder—a handsome boy, olive-skinned, dark-eyed, with rumpled black hair and a white, anxious face.

But none of them made any impression on him. He was looking at a girl in the middle of the group, a tall girl with glorious red hair and great, brown eyes, who stood staring at Dick as though she could not take her eyes from him.

Holly Inglehart!

CHAPTER 4

SHE WAS tall and thinnish and extremely pale. Her hair was almost copper color, falling in thick, glistening waves to her shoulders. There was a wistfulness, a soft gentleness, about her face, and at the same time, a kind of stern determination. Her eyes, Jake noted with approval, were wide and deep and brown.

Dick had picked well. Too bad this murder had to happen. She would make a good picture, too, in that plain gray suit with the white blouse.

She was trying to smile at Dick.

"I didn't do it."

"Now!" said Mr. Fleck with gentle reproval.

"But I didn't do it. I woke up and—" she frowned and passed her hand over her eyes.

"Don't try to talk now," Dick advised her.

No, don't try to talk, Jake thought, because every time you open your mouth, Hyme Mendel's going to put your foot in it.

"You don't believe me," she said dully, "nobody believes me."

Jake caught himself starting to say, "I believe you." Funny thing, he did, too. And he hadn't heard her story yet, not from her own lips.

It was something intuitive, something that bothered him

and that he couldn't explain. You met so damn many girls in this orchestra racket that you got so you could spot the nice ones first try. This was, obviously, a nice one. And nice girls didn't go around murdering people.

But that wasn't the reason. It was something stronger, something that couldn't be explained away, or reasoned with. He knew that the thin, red-haired girl had told the truth in her fantastic story. Everything had happened just as she said it had. Jasper Fleck and Hyme Mendel and Andy Ahearn were being logical and wrong.

"Nobody believes me," she said again. Her voice was flat and tired.

Dick was trying, clumsily, to comfort her. It seemed to Jake that comfort wasn't in order. That girl wasn't asking for comfort. You wouldn't see tears on that face. She had learned years ago to keep them back. Learned it the hard way, too. Now she was really on a spot, and she was the calmest person in the room. They were going to drag her off to jail and she'd be tried for murder and possibly convicted. Probably would be, with the evidence they had against her. And she hadn't murdered Alexandria Inglehart and she knew she hadn't.

She was standing there right now, Jake knew, with a big lump of ice where her stomach ought to be, with her mind repeating over and over, "Why won't anybody believe me? Why won't anybody believe me?" And she was as unruffled as though she were about to take off for a day's shopping tour.

Dick believed her guilty, Jake could see that he did. He didn't want to believe it, he was fighting against it, but everything pointed to it, and he couldn't help himself. Hyme Mendel believed it, and Jasper Fleck, and Andy Ahearn from the sheriff's office, and Al Hedberg. They all believed she was guilty, yes, and so did her own brother, Glen Inglehart. Only he, Jake Justus, knew that she was not, knew that it simply wasn't, couldn't be possible.

He cleared his throat demandingly. "Anyone mind if I look around a bit?"

"Go ahead," Hyme Mendel said absentmindedly.

Andy Ahearn grinned at him. "I'll take you on a personally conducted tour myself."

They went into the dark and ugly hall, up the massive staircase.

"Who are these Ingleharts?" Jake asked.

Andy seemed surprised. "Old family of Maple Park. Very high-hat. George Inglehart, he built the house. Sixty, seventy years ago, I guess. The old lady lived here all her life. She was a tough old biddy if God ever made one." He paused at a closed door where a bored policeman stood on guard. "This is the room where it happened. Want to go in?"

"Sure," Jake said calmly.

Another bored policeman was in the room where Alexandria Inglehart's body still sat in the chair before the window. It was an immense room, yet singularly crowded. Oversized yellowish flowers chased each other around a papered frieze; the walls below it were covered with pictures: paintings, prints, lithographs. No photographs, though. Jake wondered why. Despite the room's size, the furniture all seemed too large—a great bed of bright tan wood, huge chairs, heavy tables. Certainly it must have all been too large for the late Alexandria Inglehart.

"Got to get more pictures of her before we move her," Andy explained, adding, "she ain't all thawed out yet. When we got here early this morning, she sure was froze."

Jake looked at the withered body that still sat propped up,

shrunken and colorless, dressed in a stiff, pale lilac silk, in her invalid's chair. There were many glittering rings on the thin old fingers.

There were three marks on the pale lilac silk.

"She didn't bleed much," Andy remarked laconically.

Jake admired the delicate Florentine handle of the knife, left there for the photographer.

"Where'd the knife come from?"

"Old dame's paper cutter," Andy told him. He pointed at one of the wounds. "Hedberg says that's the poke that done it. The other two were made afterward. Died quick and easy. No struggle. Maybe she was asleep. Or else she knew who it was and didn't suspect what was coming. Naturally she wouldn't expect her own niece to come in and murder her."

He sighed deeply. "You still with the *Examiner?*"

Jake shook his head. "Working for the guy downstairs. Dick Dayton. Press agent and manager."

"So!" Andy made a sympathetic whistling sound. "Tough on him all right. Nice-looking babe, too." He coughed. "Still, I guess you have friends on the papers—"

"I'll tell them you're running for sheriff next term and to give you a break," Jake promised.

"How'd you know?" asked Ahearn in genuine surprise.

Jake disdained to answer.

No, he could learn nothing from the withered and colorless body of Alexandria Inglehart. Nor could he learn anything from the gloomy, overdecorated room. The old woman had been sitting by her window and someone she recognized, had come into the room and stabbed her three times with her own Florentine paper cutter, and then had opened the window and gone away. That had happened at three o'clock, and later a red-haired girl had come into the room and found the old woman dead, and fainted away at her feet.

That was what had happened.

But how could he prove it had happened that way?

He walked to the window, closed now, and looked out. In the distance he could see the lake, gray and sullen, filled with bobbing cakes of dirty ice. There was a wide expanse of snow, great clumps of dark trees. All it needed to be complete, he thought, would be a few ravens flying overhead.

Today Dick and Holly were to have started on their honeymoon. An elopement. Orchestra leader and heiress. Angry aunt in background. A beautiful story Pictures all over the front page of the second section.

Well, there were going to be front-page pictures, all right. Plenty of them. But they'd be illustrating the wrong story.

Jake turned back to the room and saw the clock—Alexandria Inglehart's little French clock, in the shining bell glass, with its hands stopped at three o'clock. It reminded him of something.

"What about the alarm clocks she heard?"

"Hell," said Andy Ahearn in disgust, "there never were no alarm clocks. We did everything but take up the floor this morning. Naw, either the girl is lying, or she's ratty."

Wonder where they're hidden, Jake thought, and suddenly realized how completely he believed Holly's story.

"Look here," he said to Andy Ahearn suddenly. "Maybe I'm not the one to ask. But don't people leave fingerprints on things in Blake County?"

"*Her* fingerprints on the knife," Andy said crossly. "None anywhere else. What'dya think we've been doing here all morning, anyway?"

"How many questions do I get?" Jake asked interestedly.

"She *says* she started to pull out the knife before she fainted," Ahearn added scornfully. "But that's all the fingerprints there were."

"None on the clocks?"

"None on the clocks or the window frame or anywhere else, and if you can think of a place that we haven't tried I'll buy you a drink and charge it to Blake County. She must have wiped them off everything but the knife."

"She was calm enough to wipe fingerprints off everything *but* the knife, but still so upset that she fainted," Jake said in disgust. "And why didn't she wipe off the knife while she was about it?"

"How should I know what a girl will do?" Andy asked protestingly.

"Why don't you write to Dorothy Dix?" Jake asked. He sighed deeply. "That window could have been opened by someone who wanted to get in or out."

Andy Ahearn nodded. "We thought of that too. But we haven't thought of anyone who wanted to get in or get out."

"Footprints under the window?"

Andy grinned. "Look for yourself."

Jake looked. The ground underneath the window was covered with a smooth, unbroken expanse of snow.

"Footprints!" said Andy Ahearn nastily, "footprints, when it started snowing about midnight and kept up till six or seven this morning!"

Jake thought of an impolite name for Andy Ahearn, remembered that it would be disrespectful in the presence of the late Alexandria Inglehart, and stored it away for future reference. He cast one final despairing look around the room. It had nothing to tell him, nothing at all.

"Let's go downstairs," he said wearily.

The dark-haired boy was waiting for him in the hall.

"You're Dayton's manager, aren't you?"

Jake nodded.

The boy took a long breath. "I don't know what to do. I've got to do something. But I don't know what. What does one do at a time like this? There's a lawyer who looks after the estate, but I don't imagine he's had any experience with murder. I don't know what to do. But I've got to get Holly out of this. Even if she did it, I've got to get Holly out of this."

Jake looked at him sympathetically. "Want me to help?"

"But what can you do? What can anyone do?"

"I'll get her a lawyer," Jake told him, "a lawyer who could get her out of trouble if she'd committed a mass murder in an orphanage, with seventeen policemen for witnesses."

Glen Inglehart looked at him gratefully and mopped his pale forehead. "Things like that happen to other people. You read about them in the paper every day. But when they happen to your own family—you know what I mean."

"Sure," said Jake awkwardly.

Glen hesitated a moment as though he wanted to say something more, didn't, and moved slowly away.

Before Jake could follow him, a rabbity, white-faced little man popped into the hall, stared at him, popped back behind a door, stayed out of sight for a moment, then slowly, hesitatingly, came back into the hall. He was a homely man, with startled blue eyes and mouse-colored hair. He looked, Jake thought, as though someone had just cried "Boo!" at him.

"Did you want something, sir?"

Jake nodded. "You must be Parkins"

The man nodded. "Yes, sir."

"I'm Jake Justus. I work for the man who's married Miss Inglehart. I'd like to find a telephone."

Parkins seemed to relax a little. "Yes, sir. You'll have to come
downstairs, sir. There's only the one telephone in the house, and
it's in the hall by the kitchen."

Jake followed him down the stairs, wondering why there
would be only one telephone in a house the size of a small hotel.
At the telephone he had a few words with a man named John
J. Malone, and decided that for the moment that was all he, or
anyone, could do.

But as he started back to the library, for one instant he saw
the tall, angular woman who had let him into the house. She
was, he decided, Nellie Parkins.

There was also, he decided, something very wrong with her.

Little Parkins, a naturally timid soul, was startled and anxious. That was normal enough. But while the pasty white face of
Nellie Parkins was blank and wooden, the look in her eyes was
one of pure, stark terror.

CHAPTER 5

HYME MENDEL, district attorney of Blake County, had always been a little inclined to hate everybody. In fact, he had been born just a bit angry. He was an exceptionally bright young man, and he had been aware of it ever since he brought home his first report card. But in his early life, no one seemed to notice it. The Ingleharts and other residents sent their clothes to be cleaned and pressed at his father's little shop and spoke in a kindly tone to young Hyme when he delivered them. But no one paid any other attention to him.

He was honest as well as bright, and his sense of justice was almost as furious as his sense of injustice. At heart, he was a kindly young man, but the same generous providence that had seen him through law school and made him district attorney of Blake County had dumped Maple Park's first murder in years right on his lap. Moreover, it had landed that murder among the Maple Park residents he hated most.

He felt that he should have enjoyed the situation. Instead, he was annoyed and irritated and a little hurt. He hated these people who had always ignored him.

He hated little Parkins who had seemed to imply that he, Hyme Mendel, should have used the rear entrance.

He hated Holly Inglehart, so cool and poised and perfectly at home in surroundings that bothered him in spite of himself.

And, finally, he hated poor Jasper Fleck with a positive fury because he considered the venerable chief of police of Maple Park a stupid fool who liked nothing better than to kowtow to these people.

Well, he, Hyme Mendel, was going to be different. This Inglehart girl wasn't going to be treated any differently from any other criminal. These people weren't any better than he was. He had as much right to be in the Inglehart library as anybody.

He wished he'd worn his other suit.

The situation was a serious strain on his knowledge of etiquette. How did one ask a young lady to come along on a murder charge? Especially one of the social standing of the Ingleharts?

Even Andy Ahearn was a little embarrassed. He started to say, "Come along, sister," and then stopped short.

Holly came to their rescue. "I'm quite ready to go," she said in a clear voice, smiling at them as though to indicate that she understood their feelings perfectly, knew they were only doing their duty and that the situation was an awkward one. "I'm ready to go any time."

Glen turned even more pale. "Do you have to do this? I mean, is it absolutely necessary?"

"I'm afraid so," said Hyme Mendel briskly.

"Look here," Dick said suddenly, "look here. You can't take her to jail. I won't—"

Holly interrupted him. "There's no sense making a fuss about it. It's all a silly mistake and it's going to be straightened out. Just don't worry about it."

At that moment a girl swept into the room with the velocity, and about the same effect, of a small cyclone. She, too, was tall, thinnish, but where Holly was gentle and appealing, this girl seemed made of ice and steel. Her hair was ash blonde, almost white, combed sleekly back from her ivory-pale, finely modeled face. Her eyes were blue and brilliant. She was dressed informally in galoshes, fur coat, and blue satin house pajamas.

"What in hell goes on here? The place is crawling with cops, and Nellie comes over with some insane story about Holly murdering Aunt Alex—God knows it was a good idea if she did— and—Glen, explain this to me."

They stared at her.

"And just who," asked Andy Ahearn irritably, "might you be?"

She seemed amazed that anyone should fail to recognize her.

"My name's Helene Brand, my fat friend—if that means anything to you."

Evidently it did. They looked at her with a sudden deference. Jake wondered where he had seen her picture.

"Are you taking her to jail?"

Mr. Fleck cleared his throat, apologetically. "Well you see, Miss Brand—"

"*Damned fools!*"

"It's all right, Helene," said the other girl. "It's all right. It's a mistake. It'll all be straightened out. Please don't worry. I shan't mind being in jail. Really I shan't. After living in this house all my life, it might be a pleasing novelty." She turned to smile at Andy Ahearn. "Shall we go?"

It might have been a royal command. Jake repressed a sudden impulse to applaud.

Jasper Fleck began to bustle. He gave a dozen orders to the

policemen who were remaining in the house, nodded amiably to Jake, and began shooing everybody toward the door. In a moment the heavy door of the house had closed after them.

Holly turned to wave. " 'By, Dick. See you in jail!"

Then she was gone.

For the first time Dick seemed fully to realize just what had happened. He began running down the snow-covered walk. Jake caught his arm.

"Where do you think you're going?"

"Let go of me, damn you. I'm going with her."

"Oh no, you're not!" As Dick started to swing at him, Jake pinned the young man's arms in an iron grip. "You'll run into a flock of reporters and this is no time or place to have your picture taken."

"She needs me!" Dick roared.

"Not in the Blake County jug, she doesn't!"

They glared at each other.

"If you'll keep your head," Jake added, "you can be of some help. I know what I'm doing."

Dick's opposition seemed to collapse suddenly. "Okay."

"That's better."

"What are we going to do?"

"Go back to town," Jake said gloomily, and added, "I knew we should have kept that cab."

They went down the snow-packed walk in silence. There was not a cab in sight, the street was quiet and deserted. For a few minutes they waited, stamping their feet in the snow.

"Better start walking," Jake suggested, "unless you want to go back to the house and phone for a cab."

Dick shook his head.

"Then we walk."

At that moment a long, sleek car stopped beside them, its door opened and the blonde girl leaned out.

"Hey, youse guys. Get on board. I'll drive you down to the Loop."

Jake felt her bright eyes run over him from head to foot. It bothered him a little. He felt as though she were undressing him, there in the snow. A hell of a thing to be thinking about, with Dick in a jam like this!

They climbed in gratefully, wedging into the front seat. She started the big car and began piloting it expertly over the ice.

"So you're the man Holly married."

Dick roused himself with a start. "Yes."

They drove in silence for a moment.

"I thought you were."

Another silence.

"Drink?"

Jake gasped, collected his thoughts. "Invariably."

She laughed. "Reach in the side pocket. No—this side. I thought it might be a long, cold ride into town."

Jake beamed approvingly at her. "There's a certain Florence Nightingale touch about you that's beginning to grow on me."

She laughed again. "No glasses, though."

"Well," he said, "you couldn't have everything. It wouldn't be fair."

He passed the bottle to her, watched admiringly as she tilted it up and drank deeply without allowing the big car to waver more than a little on the icy pavement. Then he handed it to Dick, who shook his head, finally lifted it to his own lips, sighed, and closed his eyes happily.

It seemed to him that a fog was beginning to lift from his brain.

"And now," the girl said, "how in God's name are we going to get Holly out of this mess?"

"I've had tougher assignments. Don't worry." Jake spoke with serene confidence.

He was pleasantly conscious of the pressure of her arm against his side when the wheel turned. They drove along the lake shore, on roads as smooth and treacherous as glass, watching the great grimed cakes of ice that bobbed up and down in the gray lake. Dick was silent beside them, staring straight ahead. After a few miles, they ignored him.

"If she did do it, I don't blame her," said Helene crisply, skidding the heavy car around a sharp curve, while Jake held his breath.

"That's fine," said Jake, "now all we have to do is get you on the jury."

"Wonderful," she told him. "I'll wear black and tell them about Aunt Alex."

"Aunty an old hell cat?"

"And then some." She missed a tree superbly. "Give me a drink, I'm nervous. She took Holly and Glen to raise when they were babies. Their mother was her younger sister. Must have been quite a gal. Aunt Alex was years and years older. Anyway, she raised her too. I'd say she had some sort of a—well, some sort of a complex about her."

"Holly's mother?" asked Jake, nursing the bottle of rye.

That's right. Only she wasn't Holly's mother then. Well anyway, she—Holly's mother—got fed up with the quiet life, I guess. Aunt Alex practically kept her wrapped in cotton wool. And that's no life for a lively gal."

"So she ran away with a traveling salesman," Jake said dreamily, wondering if Helene had ever been kept in cotton wool, and again pleasantly conscious of the arm.

"Practically the head of the class. Only he was a vaudeville actor. A bum one, too, I guess. Aunt Alex all but died of it. Said 'Sister, stay 'way from my door,' or words to that effect."

"Old stuff." They were getting into heavier traffic and Jake could feel his hair slowly turning gray. At intervals the car would slip sideways, slide halfway down a block, and miraculously right itself.

"And then she had twins and died."

"Holly's mother?"

"Naturally. And Aunt Alex relented. She fairly oozed family pride anyway. So she wrote to Papa and said that if he'd agree never to see the twins again, she'd raise 'em and make 'em her heirs. After all, they were Ingleharts and therefore sacred. So they lived with her ever since. I guess she gave their old man a bunch of dough to stay out of the picture."

They wove their way through Evanston, discarded the empty bottle at Rogers Park, bought a full one at Wilson Avenue, and turned into the outer drive, where Helene drove with absent-minded enthusiasm between cars and taxicabs. Jake wondered if he dared put a hand on her blue satin knee.

"Still old stuff," he said after a while. "I don't see any motive for murder in that little tale. At least a girl wouldn't ordinarily murder an old aunt just because that aunt had adopted her and brought her up and agreed to leave her a cut of the family dough."

"Holly had plenty of motive," said the girl grimly, braking furiously for a stop light. "And they'll see another motive, too, that isn't really there at all."

"I can see you're going to be a big help," Jake said. "To the prosecution. But go on. Tell all."

"Aunt Alex would have disinherited Holly the minute she knew about this insane—I beg your pardon, Mr. Dayton—this marriage of hers. She didn't want Holly to marry anyone. And a band leader! God! I don't know if Holly knew about that, but if she did—"

"She did know about it," Dick spoke up suddenly out of a trancelike silence. "She did know about it. We talked it over. She knew she was cutting herself out of a fortune if she married me, but she didn't care. She knew I could support her. She didn't care about the money."

"It's going to be hard to convince a jury that she didn't care," said Jake very gently, "especially if she knew that she'd be cut out of the old dame's will. No, that doesn't do her any good, not any good at all."

"Oh God," said Dick, and again, "oh God!"

"Don't do that!" said the girl sharply.

They spun west into Wacker Drive, turned south again, swung suddenly into a parking lot, struck a patch of ice, skidded around once, grazed the corner of a filling station, and came to a full stop beside a startled attendant. Jake reached for a cigarette, his hands shaking.

"Baby," he said admiringly, "baby, that was as skillful drunken driving as I've ever seen."

Dick roused himself again. "What are we going to do?"

"See a lawyer, of course," Jake told him. "John Joseph Malone."

"I know him," said the girl. "I mean, I know who he is. He defended that hammer slayer last summer. Got him off, too."

"That's the one."

They climbed out of the car.

"Well, thanks for the ride."

"Whoa. I'm coming with you. I'm in this party too."

Jake glanced dubiously at the blue satin house pajamas. She looked down at her ankles, grinned understandingly, and deftly rolled up the offending pajama legs, anchored them with the garters that held up her skin-colored stockings, wrapped her fur coat around her, and smiled triumphantly.

"What the well-dressed girl will wear to a lawyer's office!"

As they walked through the lobby of the office building, Dick stopped suddenly.

"But Jake. What's the use of going to see him?" He paused, gulped. "She may be guilty. It's horrible, but it's true. She might be."

Jake looked at him affectionately. "That's right. That's just why we want John J. Malone!"

CHAPTER 6

JOHN JOSEPH Malone did not look like a lawyer. A contractor,
or a barkeep, or a baseball manager, perhaps. Something like
that. At first sight he was not impressive. He was short, heavy—
though not fat—with thinning dark hair and a red, perspiring
face that grew more red and more perspiring as he talked. He
was an untidy man; the press of his suits usually suggested that
he had been sleeping in them, probably on the floor of a taxicab.
His ties and collars never became really close friends, often not
even acquaintances. Most of the buttons on his vest were un-
done, and almost invariably he had one shoelace untied.

His courtroom manner was spectacular and famous. It was
hardly because of his voice, which had once been publicly described (and by Jake Justus, too) as sounding like a pair of old
rusty gates swinging in the wind. His gestures were simple; he
had two. He pointed a dramatic finger or pounded a dramatic fist. He also wiped his red face with a soiled and crumpled
handkerchief every five minutes, or whenever a pause for dramatic effect was indicated.

Crowds gathered in the courtroom whenever John Joseph
Malone appeared to plead, argue, reason with, and occasionally
insult a jury that sat back and purred like twelve cats in a basket.

A witness facing cross-examination at his hands was usually reduced to a state of complete nervous collapse before the short, untidy man had even opened his mouth.

He had nothing but contempt for all but a rare few of the criminals he defended and saw acquitted, and no sympathy. Yet he worked unceasingly, amassing a considerable fortune in the process, at turning clients who were indubitably criminals loose upon society. It was not from any liking for the criminals. It was simply that he had even less liking for society. He always assumed that the words from a witness' mouth were perjury, unless he had put them there himself. He expected his friends eventually to double-cross him, and was neither surprised nor hurt when they occasionally did. Yet this did not interfere in the least with his very sincere liking for them.

He was genuinely interested in the three people who sat in his office: Jake Justus, casual, lazy-eyed, drunken; Dick Dayton, white-faced and distracted; and the exquisite blonde girl who sat nervously lighting one cigarette after another and wondering if she dared take off her coat, blue pajamas or no blue pajamas.

It was Jake who told him Holly's story as he had heard it from Jasper Fleck—the dream, the clocks, the discovery of the body. The little lawyer nodded his head.

"Insanity," he said tersely.

Jake Justus frowned uncomfortably. "It's just that things don't match up."

"Match up? What doesn't match up?"

"Oh, different things."

"Well, what things?" Malone asked.

"The phone call, for one thing. If she was there all the time, how could she have phoned from somewhere else, and if she wasn't there, where was she? If she was in bed, how could she be out of the house? If—perhaps," Jake said lamely, "we'd better get some of this straight."

"It might help," said Malone severely. He managed to find a large, clean sheet of paper without calling for his secretary's help.

"All right," he said, "first—"

"First," Jake said, "Glen goes to bed. Parkins has gone to bed. Mrs. Parkins has gone to see her daughter. Presumably Holly is in bed. The old lady was sitting up in her room. Mrs. Parkins was to put her to bed when she came home. Old lady was something of a night owl. Then. Glen gets a phone call from Holly, who claims to be at St. Luke's Hospital. Now—" he paused and thought for a moment. "Where was she when she made the phone call?"

"Where did she say she was?"

"She says she didn't make it. She was in bed and asleep."

Dick frowned. "But Parkins told you that when he was in her room, she wasn't there, and her bed—"

"I'm getting to that."

"Is there an extension phone in the house?" Malone asked.

Helene shook her head. "The only phone is downstairs. Aunt Alex wouldn't have an extension. Thought they were a damned nuisance, all telephones."

"They are, too," Jake said.

"Of course," Dick suggested miserably, "she could have been phoning from a corner drugstore."

Malone nodded thoughtfully.

"Or," said Jake suddenly, "it may not have been Holly who called."

"Someone imitating her voice?" Helene asked.

Malone nodded again. "A possibility."

EIGHT FACES AT THREE · 45

"The point is," Jake said, "first, was it Holly who called? If not, who? And where was she when that call was made? Hiding somewhere in the house? Second, if it was Holly, where was she? Phoning from a corner drugstore? *Where?*"

"She claims she was asleep," Dick said.

"Second problem," Jake went on. "Her story is—that she went to bed early and went right to sleep. Woke up at some indeterminate time after three. She got up to find out the time— heard alarm clocks ringing—"

"Or thought she did," Malone put in.

"Well—anyway, she found Glen gone and his bed not slept in. Looked in the Parkins' room—found them both gone, and the beds not slept in. Went into her aunt's room, saw the body, and fainted. The story," he said wearily, "the story ends here."

"I couldn't have thought of a better one myself," said Malone coldly.

"Now. Glen had gone to bed. Parkins had gone to bed. When Parkins went into Holly's room he found that *she* was gone, and *her* bed hadn't been slept in. There's something that doesn't jibe."

Malone wiped his face. "Unless Glen and this Parkins made up their beds after getting out of them—before going down to the hospital after the girl—their beds would have been slept in."

"Oh, you do see it, too."

"And her bed—"

"Hadn't been slept in when Glen and Parkins left the house."

"The whole thing's impossible," Malone said.

"Look," said Helene suddenly, "what was the condition of the beds when Glen and Parkins came back?"

"What do you mean?"

"Which beds *had* been slept in?"

"I see," said Jake slowly. "If Glen's bed and Parkins' bed hadn't been slept in—then either they weren't in bed when the call came from Holly—or someone romped around the house making beds while they were away."

"You get the idea," said Helene.

"And if they had been slept in," Jake continued, "then either Holly is lying or crazy or someone went around mussing up the beds while Glen and Parkins were away, and while she was— where was she?"

They looked at each other in open bewilderment.

"Anyway," said Helene, "it's simple enough to find out. I'll phone Nellie. She'll know."

"Approved," said Malone. He pointed to the phone and turned to Dick.

"A hell of a thing to happen," he said sympathetically.

Dick set his jaw hard. "The old woman deserved it."

Malone nodded vigorously. "A lot of people do. If half the people who deserve murdering were murdered, the problem of overcrowding would be solved. Still—" he paused to wipe his face again. "Tell me. Did she ever seem at all strange—well— not quite herself—queer—?"

"No. Never. Nothing like that."

"Hell," said Malone, "that's no good."

"Of course—" slowly. "She had been under a terrible nervous strain. Her Aunt Alex—she wasn't human to the girl. She—"

"Was trying to make a slave of her?"

"Yes—yes, that's it—"

"Tortured her—mentally—"

"Yes—yes, and—" Dick began to have a faint idea of what

happened to witnesses when Malone got them on the stand. "What am I saying? I mean—" He broke off, stammering.

Malone beamed. "That's all right. That's wonderful. We've got a case."

And then Helene put down the telephone.

"Well?"

"The beds had *not* been slept in."

They looked at her a little blankly.

"Or if they had been slept in—someone had made them."

"*All* of them?"

"Yes, all of them. Glen's, Parkins', and Holly's."

There was a long silence.

"But the thing's insane!" said Jake stupidly.

"If Glen's bed and Parkins' bed hadn't been slept in," Malone said slowly, "part of the girl's story appears true. About going in their rooms and finding them gone. But her bed hadn't been slept in either. And according to her story, she was in bed and asleep and—no, it doesn't jell."

"You're missing one thing," said Helene suddenly. "Holly did go to bed last night, just about the time she said she did."

"How do you know?"

"I was there."

"You—what?"

"I put her to bed," said Helene calmly. "Just before ten o'clock. I'd run over to return a book I'd borrowed, and she was just getting ready for bed. She looked terribly tired, almost groggy—I tucked her in and turned out the light, and then nipped back home again."

Malone fixed his eyes on her. "Tired? Groggy? Anything else?"

Helene stared at him. "Oh! I see what you mean. Yes, damn it—she was acting queerly. It's hard to explain exactly—but—no, not like herself—" Her voice trailed off into a thoughtful silence.

"Perfect!" said Malone happily. "Absolutely perfect!" He wiped his forehead meditatively.

"You don't get this at all," said Jake Justus suddenly. "You're all going on the theory that Holly did murder the old girl, and she was nuts when she did it. Well, she didn't. And she wasn't nuts. She's as sane as any one of us here and probably—" with a reflective eye on Helene—"a damned sight saner."

"You mean she didn't do it?" said Malone.

"You're dead right, sweetheart. You're seeing the picture from the wrong side, that's all. Get this fixed in your mind right now. Holly isn't guilty!"

John J. Malone looked at him with disgust.

"Hell's bells!" he said icily. "If the girl's not guilty, what in the name of God do you want a lawyer for?"

"Talk to her yourself," Jake said. "You'll see. Her story may sound crazy as hell and it may sound false as hell, but it's true. And she's sane."

"You mean you believe all that stuff about the clocks, and her being asleep all that time and the beds not being slept in?" Dick asked slowly.

"I believe she's telling the truth," Jake told him. "There's a lot that she doesn't know about what happened. But she's telling the truth about what she does know, and it's the key to something. Remember, the beds hadn't been slept in."

"Hers wasn't either," Malone reminded him.

"I know it. And that's significant too. I don't know how, but it is. I don't know what it means, but it means something. And her dream. It means something too. I don't know what. But something."

"You're drunk," Dick said irritably.

"I'm not having hallucinations, if that's what you mean, unless you could call her one—" jerking a thumb at Helene, "and you're seeing her too."

"Jake thinks better when he's drunk," Malone said from long experience.

"Let's hope you do too," said Jake savagely. "Go out and see the girl. She's your client."

"All right, Galahad," Malone said, looking under the desk for his hat.

"I'll drive you out there," Helene offered. "Drive all of you out there."

Jake paled. "I'm a brave man," he muttered, "but riding with you strains my courage to its ultimate limit."

She wrinkled her nose at him. "I'll feel perfectly safe, driving with a lawyer in the car. Malone here could get us out of anything."

"Not out of the Blake County morgue, he couldn't," Jake said indignantly.

"I'm coming with you," Dick said.

"Like hell you are. It's too damned hard to find a good band to manage these days. You won't risk your neck in this woman's car if I have anything to say about it. You couldn't do any good out there anyway."

"But I ought to be with Holly."

"The chances are they won't let you see her," Jake scowled at him with affection. "There's nothing you could do, and you have a rehearsal coming up."

"But—"

"I know," said Jake, "I know. You're thinking that you can't go through a rehearsal when you're wondering what's happening to your girl, and if you will ever see her again, and if she really did stab her Aunt Alex three times."

"Jake!" The young man's face was dead white. Then, "All right. You win."

"The show must go on," Helene told him theatrically.

"A little trite," Jake said, "but true, like most trite things."

"One drink before we go," Malone advised, his eyes on Dick. He rummaged through a filing cabinet for a bottle. They drank to Malone's success with the case, to Holly's ultimate vindication, and to Helene's driving. Then they headed north. They dropped Dick at the Casino and Helene settled comfortably in the driver's seat.

"Hold your breath, and watch a woman drive that can drive."

Thirty breathless minutes later they pulled up in front of the Blake County jail.

"If I can," said Jake in a small voice, "I'd prefer to forget the details of that ride. It would be better, I think, to pretend it never happened. Then there's a chance," he finished, "that it won't come back and haunt me."

CHAPTER 7

JOHN J. Malone had not been quite sure what to expect at the Blake County jail. North-shore debutantes were a little out of his line. An ex-Follies girl who had shot her husband in an enthusiastic moment, a gangster's sweetheart who had impetuously stabbed her rival, a perfumed blonde who had accidentally poisoned a wealthy salesman while trying, innocently enough, to rob him—these were his stock in trade. An Inglehart of Maple Park was a horse from another circus.

Or so he thought until he saw her. But one look at Holly Inglehart Dayton convinced him that any male jury would turn the lovely red-haired girl loose in twenty minutes.

He sat down, smiled his most reassuring smile, and talked with her as gently as he might have talked to a frightened child, in what Jake Justus had once called his best cellside manner.

"Remember, I'm your lawyer, my dear. I might be your second self. There's nothing you need be afraid to tell me. All I want to know is exactly what happened. Don't leave out any insignificant detail. It might be important. Everything. And the truth, no matter what it is."

She frowned wearily. "Do I have to tell it all over again? I'm so dreadfully tired." Her voice broke just a little.

"I know you are. I'm sorry to have to do this. But I'll learn more from you now than from what you might tell me tomorrow." He smiled at her, watching her closely. It was good that she was tired, near the breaking point, in fact. The barriers were pretty well down. She'd be too tired to remember to stick to her story, if it wasn't true.

"Go on, my dear."

"I—woke up. I'd been asleep. I went to bed and went to sleep, and I woke up, and—"

Little by little he worked the story out of her, to the last detail. It checked exactly with what Jake Justus had told him.

"This is all true?"

"Of course it's true." She smiled weakly. "You're my lawyer. You said you wanted the truth."

He glanced at her sharply. "But can't you see, young lady, it can't be true. Your brother and—" he paused a moment. Should he tell her? Yes, he decided, he should. He told her of the telephone call that presumably came from her, of Glen and Parkins driving to the hospital.

"But where was I?"

"That's just it. Where were you?"

Her eyes darkened. He went on.

"You may not have made that telephone call. Someone may have been imitating your voice. But if so, who? And why? And certainly you weren't in your bed when Parkins looked in your room. That was before midnight."

"But I must have been. I woke up there. Sometime after three. I know I did. I was in bed, and I got out of bed to look in Glen's room—"

"But when they came back from the hospital, your bed hadn't been slept in."

There was a mounting terror in her eyes.

"Tell me about your dream. The dream you had before you woke."

She told it, haltingly, the dream of hanging, of standing up in a coffin that was balanced on end. He shook his head.

"I can't see any meaning in it yet. But there must be a meaning. There must be a meaning to the rest of it."

Her eyes were pleading for reassurance. "Tell me. Could all of it have been a dream? My being in bed—getting up—the clocks—"

"But the clocks were stopped. That much is true."

"Yes. I know. And Glen's bed and Parkins' bed hadn't been slept in. I'm right about that, too. But—" Her eyes were like holes in blank paper. "Is it—do you think—I mean, could I—without knowing I was doing it—"

He looked at her long and searchingly. "Yes. It's possible."

"Oh!" It was only the faintest bubble of a sound.

"It's possible, but—no. I don't think it happened that way. That leaves too much unexplained. The fact is, Mrs. Dayton, no one knows, now, exactly what did happen in the house last night. And we've got to find out."

"And if you don't find out?"

"In that case, we'll go ahead on the assumption that you murdered your aunt in a fit of temporary insanity, and we'll have you acquitted on the first ballot."

"Oh no. You can't do that. Because I might have done it. It might be true. I'm—yes, I'm beginning to be afraid that it was that way."

He smiled at her as though she were a child afraid of the dark.

"Let's go back a little, Miss Inglehart—Mrs. Dayton. Yesterday you married Dick Dayton."

She tried to smile. "Was it only yesterday?"

"Yes, I know. It doesn't seem that way. But it's true. Why did you marry him secretly?"

"Because I was afraid."

"Of what?"

"Aunt Alex."

"Why? Aren't you of age? I thought so. You didn't need her money, not married to Dayton. She was a little old woman, crippled, bound to a wheel chair. Why were you afraid of her?"

"I don't know. But I was. I can't ever remember not being afraid of her."

"Was she severe with you?"

"You wouldn't call it severe. Cruel, perhaps. Though she never actually did anything to me. Even when I was a little girl, she never spanked me. Never touched me. But I was afraid of her. Terrified. She never spoke to me unkindly. But I used to wake up in the night and if I heard a step in the hall and thought it was hers, I was petrified. Then when she became paralyzed and never left her room—well, it was worse, somehow. It was worse than you can ever imagine."

It all came out in an almost hysterical rush, the old woman's heartless domination over everyone, the subtle ways in which she made her cruelty felt, the manner in which she kept the entire household in awe of her.

John Joseph Malone began to feel that, no matter who had murdered Alexandria Inglehart, it had been a good idea.

"And she would have opposed your marriage to Dick Dayton?"

"Opposed it!" The girl laughed wildly.

"Why? Because he was a dance-band leader?"

"No. Not that. Aunt Alex wasn't going to let me marry anyone."

"Oh, come now."

"It's true. She used to tell me that. Her sister—my mother—had married foolishly and broken Aunt Alex's heart, and I wasn't to be allowed to marry at all. It was—well, a kind of repayment. I was to stay single and live with Aunt Alex as long as she lived, and take care of her. She told me she'd left her money tied up so I wouldn't inherit anything if I married after her death."

"What about Glen?"

"Glen was different. Because he was a boy. She wanted him to marry. He was the last male Inglehart and that meant a great deal to her. You can't imagine how proud she was. She always hated to think that our father had been—nobody. She tried to pretend that it wasn't so, that we were all Inglehart. Especially Glen."

Malone frowned. "You had a motive all right. The question now is—who else had one?"

"I don't know."

"In your own family—in the household?"

"There's only Glen and the Parkinses. I don't think that the Parkinses were especially fond of Aunt Alex—no one was—but certainly they hadn't any reason to murder her. And Glen certainly hadn't any."

"No," said Malone pensively, "if she was going to disinherit you, he had every reason in the world for keeping her alive until she'd done it." He paused. "Well, damn it," he said explosively, "there must have been someone." He sighed deeply. "One thing more. When you went into her room—was there anything you noticed? Impressions at a time like that, no matter how trivial, are important. I mean—was there anything very much out of the ordinary?"

"Only the window being open and the clock being stopped and her being dead."

"Well, naturally. I mean—anything else?"

She thought for a long moment. "Yes, there was. I remember it now. I didn't think about it at the time because—because—but I did notice it. The wall safe. It was open. Not all the way, but the door was ajar. I'd never seen it open before. That's why I noticed it. That's the only thing."

"That might," said Malone thoughtfully, "be very important."

CHAPTER 8

JAKE JUSTUS leaned against the corridor wall and wondered why, when Blake County was filled with wealthy suburbs, they couldn't afford to paint the ceilings in the courthouse. Or why the walls had to be colored that dismal, sickly green.

He sighed deeply. Andy Ahearn's gin, drunk straight from a water glass, had left a curiously embalmed taste in his mouth. He wondered how Andy stood it. He wondered how long John J. Malone was going to stay with Holly in her cell. He wondered what Helene was doing in Hyme Mendel's office.

Now and then the door to the office would open, as clerks or typists went in or out, and he could see her perched on the edge of the desk, talking and gesturing. He could see a foolishly and happily beatific look growing on the district attorney's face.

Sometimes when the door remained open for more than an instant, he caught occasional phrases.

"It must be so exciting to do the kind of work you do—" "Being district attorney of a county like Blake must be a terribly responsible job—" "It must be awfully interesting—" "When I think of anyone actually learning all it takes to be a lawyer, I'm simply gasping."

Occasionally Jake heard Hyme Mendel answering with little purrs.

Glen was pacing up and down the long corridor. Jake estimated the distance and tried to speculate on the territory the boy would cover by the time Malone returned.

Once, as Glen passed, he caught him by the elbow.

"Listen, son. It isn't as bad as it seems."

The young man managed a limp smile. "You're right. Nothing could be this bad, and be real."

"That's the general idea," Jake told him.

But in another moment the boy had resumed his pacing. Jake sighed again and wondered if Andy Ahearn had any more gin, flavor or no flavor.

The door to Hyme Mendel's office remained open a moment longer than usual.

"You know a lot about the human mind, Mr. Mendel. I'm glad you do. It's more a case for a psychologist than a policeman."

"Now isn't that a curious coincidence," he heard Hyme Mendel saying happily, "that you should say that. Because that's my hobby. Psychology. If I hadn't studied law, I should have concentrated on psychology."

"Isn't that funny," said Helene. "I just sensed that about you."

The door closed again.

Glen paused in his pacing of the corridor. "What's Helene doing in there, anyway?"

"Probably writing a confession to the murder," Jake said wearily, as Malone appeared, mopping his face.

"Her story sounds true enough," Malone reported, "but it doesn't make sense." He pulled his necktie down from the vicinity of his ear. "Where's that blonde wench?"

At that moment the blonde wench emerged from Hyme

Mendel's office, waving over her shoulder, and murmuring something about seeing him later.

"Mr. Mendel said I could see Holly for a moment. Wasn't that nice of him?"

"Five more minutes and he'd have given you the courthouse," Jake yowled. "Ten more and he'd have had grounds for a breach-of-promise suit. Know the way to the jail?"

She shook her head.

"I'll show you, then." He nodded to Malone. "Meet you out front."

He led her through the maze of corridors to the wing of the building that served Blake County for a jail, to the little row of cells that were used for the women's quarters. Through the distant barred door he could see the red-haired girl sitting on the edge of her bunk.

He watched while the matron admitted Helene to the cell with a loud jangling of keys, and while the two girls talked. He wondered what they could be saying in front of the matron. After a few minutes Helene gave the other girl an affectionate pat, started for the door, stopped suddenly. She looked through her purse for something, appeared unable to find what she was looking for, turned to Holly. Holly nodded, fished through the heap of personal belongings on the steel table, and handed Helene a compact.

Jake scowled and remembered seeing Helene using her own compact in Malone's office. Then he wondered if it was the effect of Andy's gin, or if he had really seen Helene, her back to the matron, slipping a note in the borrowed compact.

When Helene rejoined him in the corridor, she smiled at him brightly "Yes, I did," she answered his unspoken question. "And I'll tell you why, too. But not right now."

They were at the door of the courthouse, meeting Malone and Glen, before he had time to ask anything more. Somehow they managed to avoid the reporters on the way to Helene's car.

"And now," Helene said, "we've got to find a place to talk." She drove slowly. "When in need of a quiet place to talk," she said at last, "I always recommend—" She skidded the car to a shuddering stop in front of a narrow building whose window announced tersely AL'S.

"With Holly in jail," Glen began dubiously.

"You won't help Holly any by going home to mourn for her," she told him, and led the way into Al's, through the barroom and to a secluded booth.

"Four ryes," she called.

"Coming, Miss Brand."

"Do all bartenders call you Miss Brand?" Jake asked.

"Of course not." Her voice was indignant. "Some of them know me well enough to call me Helene."

The bartender brought the ryes, beamed paternally on Helene.

"Terrible thing to have happen, Miss Brand."

"Well, at least it's livened up Maple Park a little," she told him.

He shook his head at her and went away.

"Can you get Holly out of this?" Glen asked Malone anxiously.

Malone nodded slowly and meditatively. "If nothing else will do it, an insanity defense will."

Glen groaned. "To think of Holly going through all this, being in jail, having to go through a trial—it's awful, all of it." He laid his head on his arms.

"Take your head off the table," Helene advised. "You'll get rye in your hair."

"I'd rather have rye in my hair than you," Jake murmured under his breath.

"You'll probably end up with both, at this rate," Malone told him, dropping his hat on the floor.

"Why did she do it?" Glen said. "Tell me, why did she do it?"

"She didn't do it," Jake snapped.

"How do you know?"

"It's his intuition again," Helene said.

"This isn't getting us anywhere," Malone said, setting his glass down hard.

"Glen, are you sure Holly was out of her room last night when the telephone call came, and when you and Parkins left for the hospital? Are you positive?"

Glen looked up, surprised. "Why, I assumed she was. I didn't look in her room myself, but Parkins did, and he said she wasn't there. Her bed hadn't been slept in. Why should Parkins lie about it if she really was there?"

"I don't know," Malone said patiently. "Why should he?"

"The answer is that he probably didn't," Jake said.

"What did you do when you got back to the house, after your wild-goose chase?" Malone asked, ignoring Jake.

"Why—Parkins went to put the car away—I went right up to Holly's room to see if she'd come back. Nellie went to put her hat and coat away and then went up to Aunt Alex's room. I was in Holly's room when I heard her scream."

"Holly's bed?" Malone prompted.

"Her bed? Oh. No, it hadn't been slept in."

"Well, what did you do then?"

"I went to see what made Nellie scream and there was Aunt

Alex—and Holly on the floor. I carried Holly to bed and Nellie brought her to, and I went downstairs and phoned the police."

"Tell me," Malone said lazily, "was the safe in your aunt's room open or closed?"

"It was closed."

"You're positive about that?"

"Positive. You see, when I first went in, I thought right away that there'd been a burglary and that the burglar had killed Aunt Alex and frightened Holly into fainting, and the first thing I did was to look at the safe. So I know it was closed."

"Could anyone have gotten in by the window?" Jake asked, waving to the bartender for more rye.

"I suppose so, if anyone wanted to. There's a trellis outside. But why would anyone climb in the window?"

"To murder Aunt Alex," Helene said.

"But why? I mean, Helene, it wasn't a burglar. We know that, because nothing was taken." The boy looked helplessly at Malone. "Nobody really liked Aunt Alex, but I can't think of anyone who would have wanted to murder her."

"Are you and Holly the only heirs?" Malone asked.

"Yes. We're all there is in the family."

"The only people who really gained anything by her death are you and Holly," Malone said thoughtfully.

"That's right."

"Did you murder her, Glen?" Jake asked.

"How could I have?" Glen asked wildly. "I was on my way back from Chicago with the Parkinses when—when it happened."

"Probably Parkins did it," Jake said. "These rabbity little men are always surprising you."

"You forget," Glen said, "Parkins was also on his way back from Chicago."

"Of the four people in the household," Malone mused, "three of you were away when the murder was committed. Three of you didn't have any real motive unless the Parkinses have some dark secret we don't know about."

"Say!" Jake said suddenly, remembering the look in Nellie Parkins' eyes.

"What?"

"Nothing," Jake said after a moment.

"Shut up then. Anyway, Holly was the only one who had the opportunity and the motive, if her aunt was really going to disinherit her."

"She would have, the minute she heard about the marriage," Helene said.

"Did you know Holly was going to marry Dick Dayton?" Malone asked Glen.

"I knew she was going to. I didn't know she'd done it, until this morning. She might have told me! After all, I'm her brother. And I liked Dick. I introduced them in the first place." He frowned. "I haven't been very much help, have I?"

"Not very much," Malone said.

"But you'll be able to do something?"

"I'll get her out of this," Malone said confidently. "What's more, I'm going to find out what happened. What really happened."

"Impossible," Jake muttered into his rye.

"Don't worry, I can do it," Malone told him.

"I'm not saying you can't do it," Jake said. "I'm just saying it's impossible."

"You've been drinking," Helene said severely. "And if we're through talking, Glen had better get home before somebody starts talking about that awful Inglehart boy being seen in a tavern the day after his poor old aunt was murdered."

Malone got up and vanished through a door in the back of the room after a murmured word with the bartender. Helene opened her purse and began making up her face. Jake noticed that she used her own compact. He shook his head sadly, decided against another drink, spotted a slot machine against the wall and began feeding coins into it. When the sixth nickel brought no results, he gave it up and walked back to the booth in time to hear Helene whisper to Glen, "For God's sake, don't tell him," with a kind of desperation in her voice.

Jake Justus sighed for the twentieth time that day and decided that the delightful thing about the whole case was that everyone connected with it seemed to be playing guessing games.

CHAPTER 9

THE INGLEHART house was strangely quiet as they drove up to it. One car, of a long, low, and unpleasantly suggestive shape stood parked near the side door. The clouds had lifted since morning, and the old house seemed larger, uglier, and even brighter, more virulent yellow in the sunlight.

Within, the hallway had an even more dismal and tomblike atmosphere minus the commotion of the morning.

A tall, thin man with very white hair and almost incredible dignity was waiting for them in the library. Glen introduced him as Mr. Featherstone and explained that he was the Inglehart lawyer. Mr. O. O. Featherstone, Jake remembered from some long-buried newspaper paragraph.

Mr. Featherstone looked austerely down his nose at John Joseph Malone.

"Really," he said to Glen, "you should have consulted me before you did anything. Before, for instance, engaging an attorney for Holly."

Glen looked bewildered and hurt.

"I took the responsibility of getting Malone," Jake said. "As her husband's manager."

Mr. Featherstone blinked.

"I don't think there could have been a wiser choice," Helene added sweetly.

Malone beamed at her. "You don't need to worry about a thing, Mr. Featherstone. I'll have her out of this without any trouble."

Mr. Featherstone shuddered slightly. He wore the expression of one who had bitten into a very bad oyster and was not sure of the correct procedure for its disposal. He turned to Glen.

"If your sister has committed this crime …" he began.

"If she has, it's all the more reason for getting a good lawyer," Helene said indignantly. "You wouldn't want to see Holly spend her life in jail, would you?"

Mr. Featherstone weighed the question.

"As a matter of ethics …" he began again, a trifle hesitantly.

This time it was Malone who interrupted him. "If there was such a thing as ethics among human beings, there wouldn't be any need for lawyers."

This was too much for O. O. Featherstone. "Well," he said with dignity, "if I'm intruding—"

"Not at all," Malone told him. "As a matter of fact, you're the very person I wanted to see."

The white-haired man looked at him questioningly.

"I want to know about Miss Inglehart's will," Malone said.

"I don't know," Featherstone began dubiously. "This seems hardly the time to discuss it—" Again he turned to Glen.

"Tell him anything he wants to know," Glen said. "It's to help Holly."

"Very well. But I haven't a copy of it with me."

"I'm sure you can give me an approximate idea," Malone said smoothly. "After all, you've handled the Inglehart affairs for years."

"It's highly irregular," Featherstone muttered.

"So is murder," Malone answered.

"Very well. The general settlements were along these lines. There were bequests to both the Parkinses—a thousand dollars apiece—and an equal amount to Maybell, their daughter. I was rather surprised at that, but Miss Inglehart never offered any explanation." His tone implied that he would have cheerfully died rather than ask Alexandria Inglehart for an explanation of anything. "The remainder of the estate was to be divided between Glen and Holly—but with a provision regarding the girl."

"Which was?" Malone prompted.

"It stated that if Holly were to marry after her aunt's death, her share of the estate was to revert to her brother."

"In those words?" Malone asked.

"Essentially, yes."

"If Holly married *after* her aunt's death," Malone mused. "But actually, she married before her aunt's death."

Featherstone nodded. "Yes, I thought of that, too. If Miss Inglehart had met her death night before last instead of last night, or if Holly had married today instead of yesterday, she would have been automatically disinherited. As it is, she still receives her share of the estate. I assume that Miss Inglehart felt that she would be able to prevent her niece's marriage as long as she was alive." He sighed. "But we never know, do we?"

Nobody answered this profound question.

"Of course," Mr. Featherstone added brightly, "I don't know how she intended to change her will."

Jake Justus had the feeling that even the air in the room had tensed.

"She—intended to—change her will?" Malone managed weakly, after a long pause.

"Why yes. That's why I'm here." Mr. Featherstone seemed surprised and almost wounded at their ignorance. "You see, Miss Inglehart telephoned me yesterday. Or, I should say, she had Mrs. Parkins telephone me and give me the message. She said that she wanted me to come out here today because she wanted to make a new will. But when I came out here, I found that she'd—that it was too late."

"Didn't you know about the murder until you got here?"

"Of course not," Mr. Featherstone said a little crossly. "No one thought to telephone me."

"Newspapers are also a modern miracle," Jake Justus said reflectively.

O. O. Featherstone looked hurt. "I read a news magazine every week, but the daily papers, no. I do read the London *Times*," he added after a moment.

Whatever Malone had been about to say, he evidently thought better of it. "You're telling us that Miss Inglehart was going to change her will?" he said in his gentlest voice.

"Yes. That's the message I received. Naturally I was surprised. Of course, in the light of today's events—" He paused.

"Yes?" said Malone coaxingly.

Mr. Featherstone gulped. "I can only assume that Miss Inglehart had learned of this marriage of Holly's, and intended to cut her out of the will. I do not like," he said firmly, "I *do* not like to speak ill of the dead. But I am forced to say that Miss Alexandria Inglehart was a *mean* old woman."

He looked around him, sensed the consternation in the room.

"Does that—information—help you any?" he said hopefully.

"Hyme Mendel would love it," Malone growled.

"But Holly didn't know anything about it," Glen said suddenly. "It couldn't have been a motive if she didn't know anything about it."

No one answered him.

In the pause that followed, they heard the sound of slow, heavy footsteps on the stairs. Glen, startled, turned toward the door; Malone held him back. The footsteps—they seemed to be of two men—took an intolerably long time to reach the bottom of the stairs, continued slowly and heavily down the hall, paused. A door opened and closed.

Mr. Featherstone was a little pale. He reached for his derby. "If there's nothing more I can do. I'll be going. You can reach me at my office, of course."

He left a little hastily. Jake decided that to the day of his death Mr. O. O. Featherstone would remember the time the body of a murdered woman was carried past the room where he stood listening to the footsteps of her bearers.

Glen led them, at Malone's request, to the big room so recently vacated. The bored policeman in the hall was gone now, the house seemed very still.

Nothing had been touched in the ugly and crowded room, save that the withered old body had been taken away. The big armchair still stood before the window. There was a little spot of blood on the upholstery. Not much, though.

The window that had been so inextricably open was closed now.

A leering dragon on a mustard-color Oriental screen seemed to follow them with its eyes.

"You're sure the safe door was closed?" Malone asked Glen.

Glen nodded. "Just the way it is now."

Malone sighed and said nothing. He looked around, shook his head. Evidently the room had no more to tell him than it had told Jake Justus earlier in the day.

"Might as well go downstairs," he said at last.

They started silently down the hall. Malone paused to examine a little door set in the wall.

"Laundry chute," he said laconically, peering in.

And then it happened.

"That safe—" Jake began. He never finished.

For just at that moment, Helene went suddenly mad. Without a sign of warning, she opened the little door to the laundry chute, and fairly sprang in.

They heard a very faint scream, a strange rushing sound, and then silence.

CHAPTER 10

THEY WENT downstairs in a headlong rush. Jake felt his brain whirling. Why in the name of God had she done it? A sudden suicidal impulse?

That lovely blonde body, broken and crushed!

It must have been some kind of madness.

Or was it a part of what was happening in this house?

He grabbed Glen's arm. "The opening to the laundry chute—where is it?"

"The basement. Right by the delivery door—"

Oh God, Jake thought, clattering down the cellar stairs ahead of Glen and Malone, I can't stand this, I can't stand it. Why do I have to *see* her—

Then there was the opening of the laundry chute, and there was Helene, sitting calmly on the floor, lighting a cigarette.

"No damages," she reported coolly.

Jake stared at her for a moment, and then covered the situation with a higher degree of profanity than even he himself would have believed possible. She listened without a word. In time he paused for breath, and Malone took up the refrain with new verses and a chorus.

Helene waited patiently until they had finished. Then she said, "I wanted to make sure of something."

"What, for the love of God?"

"That I could still slide down the laundry chute. We used to do it when we were kids. Remember, Glen?"

Glen nodded speechlessly, the color coming slowly back to his face.

"I wish you'd broken your neck when you were a kid," Malone said with bitterness.

"They should have kept the rest of the litter and drowned you," Jake added.

"But why?" Malone roared with an air of desperation.

"Didn't you ever have an uncontrollable desire to slide down a laundry chute?"

"My God," said Jake, "we're out here on damned serious business, and you have to go back to your childhood and play."

There was a look in her eyes that he didn't like. Something was very obviously stewing in that blonde head. He couldn't foretell what the result would be, but he feared the worst. She hadn't dived down that laundry chute for fun, no matter what she might say.

"Do you think it's fair to hold out on us, Helene?"

"I won't, for long. Let's get on with that damned serious business you were talking about."

Malone led the way back to the gloomy library, muttering rude words about blonde women.

Parkins, when that small shy man had been located, told them the story as he had told it before to Hyme Mendel. Mrs. Parkins' absence. The telephone call. Holly's bed, not slept in. Holly not in the house. The drive through Chicago over the icy streets, the return to find Alexandria Inglehart murdered, the open window, Holly stretched on the floor at her feet.

It seemed to Jake that Parkins was probing the far recesses of his mind for words to use, and then struggling to match them to what he wanted to say. Something, he decided, had frightened Parkins once and he had never recovered. He wondered if it were Mrs. Parkins.

"You know you want to help Miss Holly," Glen told him.

"Oh Mr. Glen," said Parkins desperately, "I'd give the very skin off me to help Miss Holly, and you know I would. And I can understand her reasons for doing it, though perhaps I'm not helping her by saying so, but the old lady, if you'll pardon me, was an old devil, in a manner of speaking. And especially so to Miss Holly, to my great distress, on account of being as fond of her as if she was my own daughter, and here she is in that jail without no one to look after her, and with this awful deed on her conscience, and even if you do get her acquitted, Mr. Malone, it's a terrible thing to think of Miss Holly going to her grave with this hanging over her, and her so young and pretty, too."

He wiped away an unashamed tear.

Jake decided it was the most words Parkins had said, consecutively, for years.

"Listen, Parkins," Malone said gently, "it's possible that Miss Holly didn't make that telephone call herself—that it was someone imitating her voice. Can you think of anyone?"

Parkins stared at him blankly. "Oh no, sir. That's quite impossible. Because I'm sure that no one could imitate Miss Holly's voice. Hers is a very—well, a very distinctive voice, if I may say so. And she has her own little mannerisms of speech. Oh no, it couldn't have been anyone imitating Miss Holly."

But there was something wrong about Parkins. Damn it, Jake thought, the man *was* keeping something back. And he was frightened more than he had any business to be.

"Think back over last night," Malone said. "Is there any-thing—anything at all—no matter how little—that you've not mentioned? That you've forgotten to tell—or that didn't seem important enough to speak about?"

They watched him breathlessly.

Parkins took a long time answering, finally shook his head. "Not a thing, Mr. Malone."

"All right. Is there anything else—I mean—that's happened recently—that might have something to do with the murder?"

This time Parkins' answer was prompt. Too prompt, Jake thought. "No, sir. There's nothing. Nothing at all."

"You're lying," Jake thought with a terrible certainty.

But it was impossible to pry anything more from the little man. At last they sent him for Mrs. Parkins. As Parkins reached the door, Malone stopped him with one more question.

"Tell me, Parkins. Why should Miss Inglehart leave a be-quest of a thousand dollars to your daughter?"

Parkins suddenly seemed to grow inches taller and develop a new, almost terrible dignity.

"I couldn't say, sir."

"Parkins, you're lying." This time it was Malone who said it, and aloud.

"It could be that the wrong done to my daughter was heavy on Miss Alexandria's conscience." There was an unexpected light in the mild eyes. "But that's not for me to discuss, Mr. Malone." The mask of perfect training and years of service slipped back over Parkins' face. "I'll send Mrs. Parkins to you, sir."

He was gone before anyone could call him back.

"What the devil does the man mean?" Malone growled.

No one answered.

It was only a moment before Mrs. Parkins came into the room. Malone motioned her to a chair.

Her pasty, unhealthy face was perfectly wooden, Jake saw, but she could not disguise the look of terror in her black eyes.

"Mrs. Parkins," Malone began, "yesterday Miss Inglehart sent a message to her lawyer, Mr. Featherstone. Can you tell me what that message was?"

"Yes, sir. She wanted him to come here today, because she intended to change her will."

"Is that all she said?"

"Yes, sir."

"Have you any idea how she intended to change her will, or why?"

"No, sir. Miss Alexandria was never one to talk about herself."

"When she gave you the message did she seem upset in any way—unlike herself?"

"No, sir."

"Did she receive any visitors, or telephone calls yesterday— or the past few days?"

"No, sir."

Malone scowled. "But damn it all—" he broke off. "Tell me about last night."

She told her story in as few words as possible. She had gone to visit Maybelle Parkins in Rogers Park. Late in the evening Glen and Parkins had called for her with the news about Miss Holly. After the wild-goose chase to the hospital, they had returned to Maple Park, and found Alexandria In-glehart murdered.

No, none of the beds had been slept in when she returned. No, she had no explanation for it.

No, she didn't know anything about the clocks except that they were all stopped. None of them had ever stopped before.

Yes, the safe door had been closed when she went in Miss Inglehart's room. She was sure of that.

No, she couldn't think of anyone who might have imitated Miss Holly's voice; she couldn't think of anyone who would have wanted to murder Miss Alexandria Inglehart.

"Tell me," Malone said suddenly, "why are you afraid?"

For just the barest fraction of a second Nellie Parkins seemed about to speak. It was as though words had suddenly rushed to the thin lips and died there. Then she shook her head.

"You'd be a bit frightened too, Mr. Malone, living in a house where a murder's been done."

"But you're more than a bit frightened," Malone said pensively. "What is it?" Nellie Parkins stared at him with impassive eyes.

"How long have you been here?" Malone asked.

"Since Miss Holly and Mr. Glen were babies, sir."

"And Parkins?"

"A bit longer than that, sir. I brought the babies here to this house."

"That's interesting," Malone said, looking up.

"Yes, sir. Someone had to bring them here on the train from St. Louis, where they were born. When I brought them here there was no nurse for them and I stayed on. After I married Parkins and the twins were older, I became the housekeeper. Parkins was a widower with a baby daughter when I came here. He needed someone to look after the child, and so I married him."

"Then Maybelle isn't your daughter?" Malone asked in a surprised tone.

"No, sir. My stepdaughter. But I'm sure I've been as good to her as though she were my very own child."

Jake tried to imagine the angular, hard-faced woman being good to a child.

Malone thought for a moment, then asked the same question he had put to Parkins.

"Why would Miss Inglehart leave your stepdaughter a thousand dollars?"

Nellie Parkins shook her head. "I really couldn't say, sir. She must have had her own reasons."

They couldn't get another word out of her. John J. Malone sighed heavily and sent her away.

"They know something," he said disgustedly after the woman had gone, "but only the good God knows what it is."

"Look," Helene said, "they're both fond of Holly. Fond of her—they'd die for her. I grew up next door. I've been in and out of this house all my life. I know how much Holly means to Nellie, how much she means to both of them. And I can't believe that they'd keep anything back that might help her."

"Do you also believe in the Easter bunny?" Jake said angrily. "Grow up. They sure as hell *are* keeping something back."

"Then it must be that whatever they know makes it look worse for Holly."

For that matter, Jake thought, looking at her, what are *you* keeping back, and why?

Malone sighed, looked at his watch, remembered an appointment in the Loop. "What's more," he said, "I'm going back on the train. The next time I ride in that woman's car, I'll be unconscious before I start."

Strangely, Helene did not protest. "Jake is staying out here," she announced. "I'm going to show him around a little."

Jake blinked, thought fast, and agreed.

"Meet you at your room in the hotel sometime this evening," Malone told him.

Jake followed her into the hall. "Now will you tell me what your idea was in sliding down that laundry chute?"

"Later," she said firmly.

They went down the cellar stairs and out through the rear door. It opened into a little driveway. The house, Jake observed, had been built into a hill. Here at the back of the house the hill had been cut away and the little driveway ran through a deep cut in the earth until it suddenly disappeared in a clump of trees.

"A person," said Helene thoughtfully, "a person could drive away from the house without being seen. I mean, without being seen from the house, or almost anywhere on the grounds. Notice?"

"I notice, but what the hell of it?"

"Nothing. It's interesting, that's all."

"So is *The Decline and Fall of the Roman Empire,*" Jake said in deep disgust, "but I prefer confession magazines."

"I haven't anything to confess yet."

She led him through the snow-covered yard, through an old stone gate into the estate next door, and down a little lane to a large garage. It was, he gathered, the Brand estate and the Brand garage.

There was a man there, the ugliest man Jake had ever seen. He was at least six foot three and broad as a barn, with apelike arms that hung almost to his knees. He had a wide, gorilla-like face, a broken nose, bright blue eyes, and an enormous, broken-toothed grin that he turned on the moment Helene came in sight.

"Jake, this is Butch."

They shook hands solemnly.

"Butch is a good guy," Helene said, as though the big man couldn't hear. "He'd do anything for me. He was a prize fighter and then he drove racing cars and then he got put in jail for something, and then he was a bootlegger until repeal came in and then he got in jail for something else and I got him out, and now he's my chauffeur."

They went upstairs to the living quarters of the garage, where Butch brought out a bottle of rye, and Helene promoted a storytelling contest that went on until the bottle was fairly well drained. Jake waited until then to spring some of the questions he had planned to ask Helene.

"You're planning something," he told her suddenly, "something hellish, I suspect. I want to know what it is."

She beamed at him. "It's going to be so simple. I've thought it all out. Every detail. And with Butch to help, there isn't anything that can go wrong."

"What are you going to do?"

"You mean, what are *we* going to do." She reached over and patted his cheek. "Hold your breath, baby. We're going to get Holly Inglehart out of jail!"

CHAPTER 11

It was, Jake had to admit, an absurdly simple idea. Or perhaps it only seemed that way at the time. Or perhaps it was the rye. Certainly in a sober moment he would have walked out on the party.

But with the rye under his belt, and under the spell of Helene's enthusiasm and Butch's willingness, it seemed a wonderful idea, a monumental idea, and Helene was a mental giant for conceiving it. It might easily have landed them all in jail or in the morgue. It might have muddled up the Inglehart case beyond all possible salvation. It might have caused two murders and possibly contributed toward a third. But at the moment, it was colossal.

It was necessary, Helene said, to get Holly out of jail. What she had seen or thought she had seen the night before was the key to what actually had happened. Somehow they had to find out where she had been during that three and a half hours.

Jake nodded solemn agreement.

"And if she stays in the Blake County jail," Helene said, "probably we never will find out. It's going to take long and patient talking with Holly to find out the truth. That talking has got to be done in private, too."

"Which is obviously impossible with Holly in jail," Jake said.

Helene was silent and very thoughtful for a moment. "And, too," she said slowly, "there's the possibility that we might not be successful. In finding the real murderer, I mean—if Holly didn't do it."

"You really think she did, don't you?" Jake said in a momentary flash of sobriety.

She looked at him and beyond him, her eyes very grave. "I don't know. I don't think she did. But I'm not sure we can prove that she didn't."

The point was, he gathered, that if they didn't succeed in learning what had really happened, and if Malone failed at the trial, Holly would be in the soup. Even, in that case, if chivalrous Blake County declined to electrocute a lady and an Inglehart, still Holly would be put away for a long time. Certainly they didn't want that to happen. Helene, for one, didn't believe that Holly was guilty. (Jake doubted that a little, but he let it pass.) Even if she was, the murdering of Alexandria Inglehart called for a bonus rather than a jail term. (Which Jake didn't doubt for a split second.) If Holly was safely hidden away somewhere, it wouldn't matter so much if they didn't find the real murderer; Holly could be kept hidden until things died down a little, and then smuggled out of the country.

It all seemed wonderfully logical to Jake.

"Shall we tell Malone?"

"Afterwards. Also Dick."

Jake sighed. "It's the sort of thing Dick would love. Knight rescues damsel. He plays Gershwin and Berlin, but he thinks Tennyson."

He looked at her with affectionate approval. So smart, to

think of such a scheme. It cleared everything up. The conversation with Hyme Mendel. The note in Holly's compact.

No. Not everything. There was something else he wanted to ask her about. Something she was keeping from him and from Malone. Important as the devil, too.

He wished he could remember what it was.

They poured the remaining contents of the bottle into the three glasses and drank solemnly to the jailbreak.

Eventually Butch made a trip to the kitchen and they dined on sandwiches and beer. Then Jake and Helene walked through the snow and darkness to the Inglehart house.

Glen seemed worried and very pale. "Thank God, someone has turned up. Have you seen Malone? I've tried to reach him all afternoon."

"Why? What's up?"

"They're going to bring Holly here tonight and make her go through the house. Some sort of experiment, Hyme Mendel said. He thinks that going through the house at night might make her remember something. I don't like it."

"She'll be all right," Jake told him. "They can't do anything to her."

"It seems to me that I ought to be doing more to help her. After all, she's my sister. My twin. And she's in this awful mess. I don't seem to be any help to her at all."

"You're all right," said Jake consolingly. "You're doing all you can."

"But," Glen hesitated, "there's no more reason, really, why they should suspect her of the murder than me. Except that she happened to be—well, somewhere where nobody knew where she was, if you know what I mean, and I wasn't. When it happened. You know."

"Sure," said Jake reassuringly.

"I'd rather they arrested me than Holly. I'm a man. There's, well, there's a difference. I could stand it, because I know I didn't do it."

"Do you know Holly didn't do it?" Jake asked.

"No," Glen said miserably.

At that moment Hyme Mendel, Jasper Fleck, and Andy Ahearn arrived with Holly. Helene greeted Mendel like a long-lost sweetheart, led them into the Inglehart library, and insisted on mixing a cocktail.

"After all," she told them brightly, "we are civilized people, aren't we!"

Jake decided that if she had suggested that they all go out to a barn and eat hay, Hyme Mendel would have assented as willingly.

She mixed the cocktail herself. "My own invention," she told them. "I call it Hearts Aflame."

The first taste of it convinced Jake that his ears had moved two inches farther back on his head.

They had a second and a third before starting on the rounds of the old house. Jake watched Holly closely. The girl was extremely pale and oddly quiet, as though she were walking in a hypnotic trance.

They trailed up the stairs, paused at the door of Holly's room, where she seemed to be doing her best to be Trilby to Hyme Mendel's Svengali. He watched her with the careful eye of a man who has a cross section of frogskin under a microscope.

The visit to Holly's room brought nothing to her memory. They went on to Glen's room.

Jasper Fleck, Jake decided, was a holy sight with three of Helene's cocktails under his belt.

They left Glen's room and headed for the stairs to the Parkins' room. Then everything began to happen with a breath-taking suddenness.

Helene dropped the glass she was carrying and it rolled down the stairs with a terrific clatter. For an instant everyone turned to look at her.

In that instant, with one swift motion, Holly slipped down the laundry chute.

There was a sharp cry from Hyme Mendel.

"My God, she's committed suicide!" Jake howled.

Helene gave a low moan and fainted.

"Quick!" Andy Ahearn cried. "Down the stairs!"

They started down the stairs in a mad rush. A thick Oriental rug covered the landing. Somehow Jake caught his foot in it and they all sprawled on the floor. They sorted themselves out and continued the rush. In the excitement of the moment Glen led them down the wrong staircase to the cellar and they wound up in the furnace room. That meant climbing up the stairs to the first floor (by that time Jasper fleck was on the verge of a stroke) and going down the back cellar stairs to the tradesmen's entrance.

There, to their horror, was no sign of Holly Inglehart Dayton, though the door to the laundry chute hung open.

Squad cars came with an insane shrieking of sirens, the house was searched from cellar to attic, the grounds were searched, the lake front, the driveways, the woods.

All night long the cars prowled Maple Park and its environs; all night long the police radio station blared descriptions of the missing girl.

It was no use. Holly Inglehart Dayton had vanished from sight, as completely as though the earth had swallowed her.

CHAPTER 12

SOMETIME LATER a slightly staggering couple came down the steps from the elevated station at Thirty-first Street. They turned down a dimly lighted street for half a block or so. A sleekly powerful car stopped alongside. They climbed in and the car drove on.

The big car carried a peculiar burden. In the back seat was a figure wrapped in a man's overcoat, its head and hands swathed in gauze bandages.

Jake and Helene looked at the ghastly thing and hooted with appreciative laughter.

"Butch, you did a swell job."

Holly giggled faintly behind the bandages.

They drove around for a few blocks.

"We're safe all right, Butch," Helene said. "Nobody followed us, and even if anyone had, the quick changes we made from el train to el train would have lost an efficient ghost."

In the enthusiasm of the moment Butch drove through a red light. There was a sudden horrible confusion of whistles and brakes squeaking.

"Oh, God," Helene breathed.

They pulled up to the curb and a round-faced policeman came alongside. Helene opened the door and leaned out.

"I'm sorry, officer—we're taking my husband to the hospital—he's been seriously injured—"

"I'm a doctor," Jake added, "and there mustn't be any delay in getting him there."

"Go on, go on," said the policeman, waving a hand, "but watch your driving or there'll be another accident."

They drove on down the street.

"See?" said Helene brightly.

"You're wonderful. There ought to be a Nobel prize for jail-breaking." They turned into the outer drive.

"Miss Helene," said Butch joyously, "you'd never guess what I got under them blankets on the floor."

Helene investigated.

"Judas!" she said. "Champagne!"

"I thought it seemed sort of appropriate."

"But no glasses," she said. "I suppose nobody can think of everything. Just the same, drinking champagne out of a bottle in a moving car is more than a mere accomplishment."

"I'll drive slow," Butch promised.

"Holly," Helene asked, "did you murder Aunt Alex?"

"Not that I remember," Holly said. "How long do I have to keep these damn things on?"

"Until we decide what to do with you."

They drove around Jackson Park until the champagne was gone. Then they headed north on the Drive, skirted the Loop and followed the lake shore to Lincoln Park.

"Not too far north," Helene warned.

"Look here," Jake said, "we can't just go driving her around indefinitely. For days and days, I mean."

Helene sighed. "I know. We would think of everything except how to dispose of the body."

"Couldn't you park me at a hotel?" Holly asked hopefully.

"Don't be a dope. Every hotel in Chicago has a description of you by now. And you could hardly go in wearing those bandages."

"How about rooming houses?" Butch asked.

"No good either. A description of Holly is in every newspaper."

"Well, damn it," said Helene, "we've got to do something with her. If we were back in Maple Park, I could hide her in my house forever. But we couldn't get back there."

"Isn't there some way I could get out of the city?" Holly asked.

"Remotely possible, but we want you here."

They drove in silence for a while.

"Well," said Helene, "as I said before, nobody can think of everything."

"I've thought of something," Jake said slowly, "but I don't know—"

"What?"

"She'd be perfectly safe there," he went on, "and nobody would ever need know. And certainly she'd be well hidden."

"What are you talking about?" Helene asked.

"Well, it's a little hard to explain. But it isn't far from here—just a little west of Lincoln Park—and it would be perfectly safe."

"Jake, what kind of a place *is* this?"

"It's—" he gulped. "Well, it hasn't a very good reputation, but as far as—"

Helene hooted. "Jake, where is this brothel?"

"Helene!" he said in a scandalized voice. "Such language!"

"My God," she said, "it's a perfect idea."

"Mrs. Fraser," said Jake, warming to his subject, "is an old pal. I got her out of jams no end of times when I was working for the *Examiner*. She's an honest woman with a strong sense of the conventions, and Holly will be safer there than anywhere else you could name."

"Tell Butch where to drive," Helene said, settling the matter. "Hope you don't mind, Holly."

"Not at all," came the muffled voice from behind the bandages. "At least it's better than the Blake County jail."

They drove to the address Jake gave them and waited in the car while he went in to make arrangements. A few minutes later he emerged, beaming.

"All okay. Drive around to the alley."

They left the car in the alley, went through a neat backyard and were met at the back door by a broad-faced woman with gray hair and the faintest suggestion of a mustache.

"Up the stairs, dearie. Then there won't be a Chinaman's chance of your being seen."

She led the way through a spotless blue-and-white kitchen and up what seemed an endless flight of back stairs. On the fourth floor they halted while she fished for a key and unlocked a door.

"There you are, my dear. My daughter's room, that she uses when she's home from boarding school."

"I helped get the daughter into that school," Jake whispered to Helene, "and if I told you which one it is, you'd drop dead."

It was a dainty little room with a ruffled bedspread and pink curtains.

"This is just our own little home up here on this floor," the woman went on, "and there won't a soul bother you. In case you're a bit nervous, I'll leave you the key and you can lock the door. It does get a bit noisy downstairs sometimes, but you won't notice it much, and I'll bring your meals up to you."

Holly began unwinding bandages.

The stout woman chuckled. "Those bandages! As neat an idea as you ever had, Jake Justus!"

"Don't credit me," Jake said, "it was this crazy blonde."

Helene bowed.

"Holly, would you like a drink?" Jake asked.

She nodded.

"Oh dearie," said Mrs. Fraser reproachfully. "You're much too young to be drinking. If you knew what that stuff does to your stomach!"

"Just a little one," Jake pleaded. "Remember, she's been through a terrible strain."

The woman was instantly all sympathy. "Of course she has, poor dear." She beamed at Holly. "You just wash your face and comb that pretty hair of yours. I'll have a tray up here in a minute." She left them, closing the door.

Butch beamed. "Well, Miss Helene, I guess we done it, all right."

"If we don't all draw twenty years to life for it," Jake said gloomily.

Holly began combing her hair. "What's the next move?"

"For you to get some sleep," Jake told her, "quite a lot of it. Then we're going to sit down with you and talk this whole thing through. Then you'll stay here and catch up on your reading, while we find out what really did happen last night, and then we turn up the real murderer, and you reappear in triumph and start on your honeymoon."

"Or?"

"Or," said Helene, "we smuggle you out of the country disguised as a shipment of contraband ammunition."

"Oh."

There was a long pause.

"Oh God," said Holly suddenly, and again, "oh God, if I only *knew!*"

"Stop that," said Jake.

"But I keep thinking and thinking, and I know there's something important that I've forgotten, and perhaps that's what it is. Perhaps I really did do it, and I can't remember it, and that's why my mind just keeps going on and on like this."

Helene gave her a smart slap that stopped the flow of words.

"You've got to stop thinking," Jake told her. "You're going to go to sleep and tomorrow when we talk it over, you're going to remember." He wished he felt as sure as he sounded.

Madam Fraser came back bearing a tray with a bottle, glasses, plates, and an enormous platter of cold fried chicken.

"I thought you all might be hungry." She set the tray down and looked searchingly at Holly.

"You're right, Jake," said the woman surprisingly. "She didn't do it. She's too much of a lady." She smiled at them all impartially. "Good night. I hope you sleep well, dearie. And Jake Justus, don't you forget to latch the back door when you leave."

They cleaned the tray of food and liquor and prepared to leave.

"I'll try to smuggle you some clothes," Helene promised.

Jake took the girl's hand for a moment. "Forget things, baby. Don't worry. Everything is going to be all right. I mean, *whatever* happens, everything is going to be all right."

She smiled at him gratefully. "Thanks, Jake. And when you see Dick, tell him—"

"Tell him what?"

"Oh—I don't know. Something. Tell him something."

"Okay. Good night, kid."

"Jeez," said Butch admiringly, on the way down the back stairs. "That kid's got nerve."

They drove in silence toward the Loop.

"God, what a night," said Helene suddenly. "Driving all over Chicago with an escaped murder suspect wrapped up in bandages, and finally hiding her out in a cat house. To say nothing," she added, "of the original escape. That idea about the rug on the stair landing was a stroke of genius, Jake. What a night!"

"This is only the first act," he told her, looking at his watch. "Malone is waiting for me at the hotel right now."

She nodded. "I'm playing in this scene with you." She leaned forward. "Butch, take the car home. I'll come home in a taxi, if at all." She looked at Jake. It's my hunch we'd better keep this from Malone and Dick until tomorrow. It may save a lot of explanations we're too tired to make."

"Just as you say, baby. This is your jailbreak."

"We'll have to make some excuse to Malone for being so late. I know," said Helene brightly as the car stopped in front of the entrance. "I know! We'll tell him we've been drinking."

Jake widened his eyes. "He'll never believe it!"

CHAPTER 13

"I want to go to the Casino and hear Dick's band," Helene said.

"In those blue pajamas?" said Jake indignantly. "Hell's bells, woman, don't you own any other clothes?"

They had found Malone sleeping peacefully in Jake's room, wakened him by holding an opened bottle of rye under his nose. Now they were draped about the room—Jake comfortably settled in the one easy chair, Malone sprawled on the bed, and Helene lying flat on the floor. It had, she said, a reassuringly immobile quality which the furniture lacked. It wheeled a little, but it did not spin.

"I own other clothes," she said, "but nothing as fetching as these pajamas. Still if you don't like them, I can always take them off."

"You two fools are drunk," Malone said hastily.

"'Malone says Dick's deb not guilty,'" Jake read from the pile of afternoon papers heaped on the floor, and made a mental note to keep the last editions away from Dick and Malone. He picked up another. "'Band Leader's Bride Didn't Murder Aunt, Lawyer Says.'"

"Well, is she guilty?" asked Helene from the floor.

"Of what?"

"Auntycide."

"What do you think?"

"Hell, no."

"Personally," Jake said, "I think Helene did it and she's just trying to confuse us."

"Do you confuse easily?" Helene asked in a dangerously dulcet tone.

Malone rose to his feet a little unsteadily. "I have things I ought to be doing."

"Sit down," Jake snapped. "Don't leave me alone with her."

Malone sat down heavily.

"It seems to me," he said a little severely, "that you two are taking this pretty damned lightly."

"I always take these things lightly," Helene told him. "I'm not the romantic type."

"I'm talking about the murder."

"Just a single-track mind," Jake said, digging under the pile of newspapers for the bottle. "It's over, isn't it? The old lady's dead and we can't bring her back. Personally I wouldn't if I could."

"I want to go to the Casino and hear Dick's band," Helene repeated.

"In the pajamas?"

"In them or out of them. Let's toss a coin, like the young man did to decide whether to visit a phrenologist or go to see his girl."

"What have you got on under them?" Malone asked in a disinterested tone.

"You're not on a witness stand," Jake reminded her. "Don't let him intimidate you."

"I don't intimidate worth a damn." She managed to get on her feet. "But watch this." She pulled the pajama legs loose from her garters so that they fell gracefully about her ankles, wrapped her coat about her person and stood artfully posed like a debutante about to be photographed at the opening night of the opera, "Do I have on an evening gown?"

"You have," said Jake. "By God, you have."

"These pajamas have been everywhere," she told him convincingly.

She began intensive operations with facial cream, powder, an eyebrow brush, and a deadly looking lipstick. They watched until she folded the contents of a small-sized beauty parlor into her handbag. "Tell me, John Joseph, did Holly do it or didn't she?"

"No," said Jake Justus.

"You're a hopeless minority," Malone said.

"You damned fool," Jake said indignantly. "You heard her story."

"She was alone in the house with the old lady," Malone began slowly and a bit thickly. "Her brother and the Parkinses are gone. She hated her aunt. Had hated her for years, was afraid of her. The old woman had terrified her, had deliberately terrified this fragile, delicately reared girl. Now she approaches a crisis in her life. Something snaps in her brain and—"

"Save it for the jury," Jake reminded him.

"Shut up. Anyone looking at what happened last night, seeing it lucidly and coldly and calmly, can see it was the product of a disordered mind. The clocks. The telephone call. Making Glen's bed and Parkins' bed. Some deep psychological significance in that. Going up and stabbing the old woman three times. Why three? Opening the window. Why? And then fainting away at the old woman's feet. That's where they found her."

"You forget," said Jake, "who made her bed. She was in it when she woke up. Who—"

"She *says* she was in it."

"Damn you, Malone. We'll get another lawyer. Who made her bed? Some roving chambermaid on the loose, I suppose. Or she slept on the floor. No, Malone, it won't wash."

"I want," said Helene stubbornly, "to go to the Casino and hear Dick's band."

Dick Dayton, at the Blue Casino, led his band with an unthinking, mechanical precision. The music seemed to come from very far away, through a mist, the figures on the dance floor were so many wound-up dolls. In the intermissions he was vaguely conscious of people talking with him, but the words they said could not penetrate the fog that encircled him.

Jake had told him to see it through. Swell publicity, Jake said. Those people out on the dance floor knew what had happened—they knew that his girl, his bride, was held for murder in the Blake County jail. They knew it and they sympathized, and they saw him here in front of his band trying to act as though nothing had happened and not succeeding very well, and it was swell publicity, Jake said. The hell with Jake. He didn't have the faintest idea what the boys were playing.

Why had she done it? Or had she done it? If he only knew. If he could only talk with her again, if she would only tell him the truth. But they wouldn't let him talk with her alone. God! Would he ever be alone with her again? If they convicted her, would they allow her an hour alone with him before they led her down the corridor to the electric chair? *Christ!*

The baton snapped in his hand. Steve came up, offered to take over, he waved him away.

This was to have been their first night together. Now he was here and Holly was in a cell in the Blake County jail. Holly in a cell. Holly in a cell, perhaps for life. And he going to see her on visiting days. Perhaps after twenty years or so they would pardon her. Half a lifetime off for good behavior. Well, he'd be waiting for her—forever if he had to.

Could Malone get her out of this? Jake seemed to think so. Jake was a smart guy. Malone seemed to think so, too. The trial would be swell publicity, wonderful publicity, marvelous publicity. God, what publicity! Damn Jake Justus. Sure they'd acquit her. Malone knew his stuff. Not guilty by reason of temporary insanity. An acquittal on the first ballot. Hell, yes!

And then would she tell him the truth? Would she tell him if she'd gone up to that room and taken the little knife in her hand and crept up to the helpless old woman and thrust that knife into the withered old bosom, again and again and again?

Would he ever know?

Ah! There was Jake. Jake, and John J. Malone, and that gorgeous, beautiful, magnificent blonde wench. Not in the same class with Holly, no. But terrific. Where the hell had they all been? She looked like a queen in that evening wrap, with just enough of her blue evening gown showing. Blue evening gown hell! Those pajamas!

He began to laugh, too loudly.

Steve stepped up, took the baton from his unresisting hand, and gently shoved him in the direction of Jake's table. Dick nodded gracefully.

Easy, he kept telling himself, easy. Don't let them know, don't let them see. He pretended they were a table of important customers, smiled, bowed, and sat down with them.

"Well, how goes it?" He managed to say it casually, hoping they wouldn't have any news, no news that he couldn't bear hearing.

"Going! It's gone! We know she didn't do it. Malone isn't even going to let it come to trial." Dick didn't see the warning glance Jake gave Malone.

"Sure," Helene said, kicking Jake under the table, "she's practically out of jail right now!"

"Drink, Dick?"

"No, thanks. I'm not drinking."

"You'd better," said Malone thickly, "you'd better have one with us, to celebrate."

"Hell, yes," Jake added, "you've got to celebrate. She didn't do it. The rest is mere formality."

"—parts Benedictine, two parts Metaxa brandy, and a dash of orange bitters," Helene was saying to the waiter. She smiled briskly at Dick. "I ordered that for you, babe."

"What is it?"

"A little invention of my own. I call it the Chicago Fire."

There was no doubt she had named it correctly.

"Jake, you meant it?" Dick asked after the third Chicago Fire. "She didn't do it? You're telling me the truth?"

"You don't think I'd lie to you about a thing like this!"

Helene interrupted with a question about the orchestra. Then Jake began telling stories; John J. Malone began telling stories. Then a black-haired wench in a bright yellow dress came from somewhere and attached herself to them, especially to John J. Malone. Everything began to get a little dim.

Somehow they all got out of the Casino and into a taxi. How it was achieved, not even Jake knew. There was Brown's where Helene won six-eighty-five in a slot machine and spent it on drinks for the house; Lucky Joe's where the wench in the yellow dress and Helene insulted each other; the Blue Door where Jake lost seven-fifty at dice with the bartender; the Rose Bowl where John J. Malone got into a fight with a stranger from Rock Island.

Dick was not quite sure what was going on. It should have been a swell evening, a hell of a swell evening. But every time he began to feel a little at home in his surroundings, there was that terrible, aching remembrance of Holly in jail, Holly, his girl. And tonight, of all nights since the beginning of time!

At those times Helene would put a glass in his hand and he would drink it, Jake would remind him that they were celebrating, and John J. Malone would mumble, "Sure, we'll have her out of there tomorrow."

They went to Johnny Leyden's, where John Joseph Malone got into a fight with a perfect stranger from South Bend and lost the collar off his shirt; to the 885 Club where Dick managed to get Holly off his mind long enough to substitute hilariously at the piano; to Riccardo's, where Helene sang in a surprisingly good voice to the tinkling guitar; to a black and tan on the south side. Somewhere along the way they lost John J. Malone—they never did find out where.

By that time Dick was aware, now and then, that something was terribly wrong with his world, but it was difficult to remember what it was. Something that had to do with some girl.

They went cruising madly along the drive in a taxi, and he remembered it all suddenly and terribly, and knew that they had been lying to him all along, and there was something he wanted to tell Jake, because Jake was his friend. Then everything became very dim indeed and the interior of the taxi became a deep dark well in which he was being drowned, and he felt Jake's hand reaching out to catch him as he fell.

"We certainly took care of that situation in a hurry," said Helene, looking down at Dick. They had driven back to the hotel where, with the help of a bellhop and a taxi driver, Dick had been tucked into his bed.

Helene looked at him for a long moment.

Rumpled and pink-faced, his eyelids swollen, he looked like a small boy who had cried himself to sleep.

"He doesn't know anything about it," Helene murmured. "He'll remember, when he wakes up in the morning. He'll wake up knowing that something is wrong, but he won't know what it is, and then little by little he'll remember until it all comes back to him, all of it."

Suddenly she bent over the bed and kissed him lightly on the forehead.

Then they went across the hall, to Jake's room. Jake found two drinks hidden in a bottle tucked away under his clean socks. The room was silent, deathly silent. There had been much noise, much excitement, much disturbance. Now it was very late, and incredibly quiet.

Jake looked at the girl. What did one do under the circumstances? A Miss Brand of Maple Park was a bit outside his ken. This sharp edge of the moment stuff was always bad. What were her views on the subject anyway?

"Tell me," he said, stumblingly, and again, "tell me."

For just one moment she was sober, cold sober. Something crossed her face that hurt, that even hurt him, looking at her. He saw the same terror in her eyes that he had seen in Nellie Parkins' eyes.

"What is it?" he said sharply. "*What do you know?*"

"Don't ask that! Don't ask that again!"

"I won't." He meant it.

He looked at her closely. Her face was frozen, her eyes had a curiously jellied look.

"My God," he said to the empty air, "you're out as cold as a clam." He caught her as she fell.

He carried her across the room, deposited her on the bed, wondered what to do about, or with, the blue pajamas, decided to leave them where they were, covered her with a blanket, and began thinking about what Holly Inglehart Dayton had done or hadn't done the night before.

Sometime later he struggled out of a half doze, looked at the blonde head on his pillow, wondered whose it was and how it had gotten there, glanced at his watch. It was three o'clock.

He sat bolt upright. She opened half an eye.

"Now I remember what it was I wanted to know!"

She muttered a remark that was either highly pertinent or highly impertinent, or both. He didn't hear it.

"What stopped the clocks?"

And then, peaceably and without another word, he passed silently out.

CHAPTER 14

FOR A long time Dick Dayton kept waking up and making himself go back to sleep again. There were brief moments of hot, uncomfortable waking, the thought that there was some reason why he didn't want to wake up, and then a supreme effort that sent him back into the void.

But the moments of waking grew longer and more uncomfortable, the periods of sleeping briefer, colored with unpleasant dreams.

It was the jangling of the telephone that drove the last sleep from him. He reached for it; spoke into it irritably.

"Well?"

It was the desk clerk. "Mr. Dayton, there's quite a lot of reporters here who insist on seeing you."

"Tell them to go to hell. I'm sleeping."

He hung up the phone with an angry clatter. What in blazes did a bunch of reporters want to see him about. Was one of the boys in trouble again?

Something was wrong with his head. Something was very wrong with his head. It pained and it didn't belong to him. Somebody happening to go past his bed had had this head along with him and had left it on the pillow. Why would anybody wish such a head on him? His stomach still belonged to him, but he wasn't sure of its location. It didn't seem to be in the same bed with him—somewhere in the next room, perhaps. He didn't want to know where it was. Much better not to associate with such a stomach. Something unpleasant had been happening to it. The less he knew of it the better.

He gathered all his strength for one magnificent effort and opened his eyes. The head and stomach promptly returned and announced themselves to be his property.

What on earth had he been doing last night? It had been years since he had gone on a bender. He tried to remember. There was a dim picture of touring Chicago with Jake and some strangers—an untidy little man, a blonde babe in blue—blue what? Oh God, yes. Blue pajamas. Helene—Helene Brand from Maple Park. The untidy little man was named Malone.

He remembered everything in one terrible, overwhelming flood.

Where was Jake? Where was Malone? What time was it? Where the hell was everybody? What was happening?

Suddenly his door opened softly and Helene tiptoed in.

"Oh, you're awake."

He felt that he ought to be scandalized at her presence. Yet he hoped that she wouldn't go away. He had a growing conviction that he was not long for this world, and he wanted company when he died.

"Don't move. I know how you feel." She grinned at him. "Just the lady with the lamp. And what a pair of lamps you've got this morning!"

He managed a smile.

"Swallow this." She poked a tablet into his mouth, held a glass of water to his lips. The water tasted horrible.

"What is it?"

"It represents a few hours more sleep. By the time you wake up, everything will be all right."

"Holly?"

"She's all right. Shut your eyes."

He shut them. The darkness felt comforting. She laid a hand on his forehead; it was cool and gentle. He heard her murmuring something about Holly in a voice that faded farther and farther away as be slipped into a dream where Holly waited for him.

After a few minutes Helene slipped from the room, hung a DO NOT DISTURB sign on the door, and crossed the hall to Jake's room.

There were blankets and pillows everywhere, cigarette butts everywhere, empty glasses, empty bottles, ashes on the carpet, burnt matches scattered from wall to wall. Jake's socks on one chair, Jake's tie on another, one of Jake's shoes on the window sill, the other unaccountably missing, Helene's fur coat hanging gracefully from a floor lamp.

"He'll sleep a few more hours and wake up feeling better," she reported, looking about the room. "This place seems just a bit on the shambles side."

"It's only a shambles in old shambles town," Jake caroled happily.

"Please, Mr. Justus!" She yawned, stretched, and began intensive cleaning operations. "I'm a naturally tidy soul."

"A naturally tidy heel, you mean."

She wiped the accumulation of ashes, spilled powder, and used matches from the dresser, tucked socks and ties into drawers, rinsed glasses and set them in a neat row on the desk, straightened the bed, collected cigarette butts and deposited them in the waste basket along with a set of empty bottles, found one bottle that was half full, set it on the dresser, looked at it, and shuddered.

"You'll feel better," Jake told her. "It's all a matter of time."

He looked at her admiringly. Her delicate, almost blue-white skin was fresh and clear; her pale hair was smooth and gleaming.

The telephone rang.

"Yes?" said Jake into it inquiringly, and then, "oh. Yes. Yes. No. Yes. Oh yes." He hung up the receiver. "That was Malone. He's coming to breakfast "

"Thus carrying away the last driftwood of my reputation," said Helene thoughtfully.

"John J. won't care," Jake said, "he's ruined more reputations than you ever dreamed of having."

"I care," she said, "because I hate to be blamed for things I haven't done."

"Nobody's fault but your own," he told her. "You pass out at the damnedest times. But eventually—" He remembered something he had wanted to do since yesterday—kissed her long and enthusiastically.

There was a delicate knock at the door.

"Damn!" said Jake explosively. He opened the door to admit John J. Malone.

He looked at the little lawyer meditatively, studied the faint pinkness in his round eyes, wondered where he had been and if he had learned the name of the wench in the yellow dress. But he had no chance to ask.

"Of all the damn fool things to do," Malone said as he walked in. "Of *all* the damn fool things to do. Do you realize what you've done? Do you realize the implications of this? Do you realize the kind of a spot I'm in? Do you know what you've let yourself in for?"

He flung an armful of newspapers on the floor.

"It seemed like a good idea at the time," said Jake wearily. "One of those impulses of the moment that you can't resist."

"Where in God's name have you hidden her?"

"Won't tell," said Jake coyly.

Malone swore desperately. "Three million people in Chicago, and everything happens to me! *Where is she?*"

"Don't tell him," Helene said. She looked at Malone. "Do you really want to know?"

He thought a moment. "No, by God, I don't."

"I didn't think you did."

"What is this?" Jake asked. "A game, and what kind?"

"If I don't know where she is, I'm still in the clear," Malone told him. "My professional reputation is safe."

The word Jake used about John J. Malone's professional reputation was very very rude.

"She's in a good safe place," Helene said, "where nobody on earth could find her. When you do want to know, we'll tell you."

Malone groaned. "But how did you do it?"

Jake described the mad flight through Chicago with Holly disguised as an accident victim.

Malone sighed, swore, finally laughed. "That damn blonde wench," he said to Jake. "She'll land us all in the penitentiary before we're through."

"She'll make it worth it if she does," Jake said happily. "Give me those newspapers, and order breakfast." He read avidly while Malone talked to room service.

"Now I know how people feel about their press notices," he said at last. "Listen to this, 'Police state that the fugitive could not have been aided from outside, as no suspicious persons had been seen anywhere in the neighborhood, although a close watch had been kept. Jasper Fleck, chief of police of Maple Park, declared he is unable to tell how the young woman managed to escape from the grounds on foot. However, there appears to be no other explanation of her disappearance.'" He laughed. "Helene had that car of hers parked with a whirlwind driver who had Holly halfway to the Loop before Jasper Fleck was down the stairs."

"Of all the Goddamn crazy stunts."

Breakfast came; it made everyone feel much better.

"There's something I keep trying to remember," Jake told Malone over the last of the coffee. He rubbed one ear. "It bothers me. Something very important, too. What the hell— Oh never mind. It's going to come to me. What do we do this morning?"

"We take me to where I can get some clothes," Helene said firmly.

"I'm a little bored with those pajamas myself," Jake told her. "But I wasn't talking to you."

Malone frowned. "We're going back to Maple Park. The Parkinses are keeping something back and I've got to know what it is. And I want to check on Featherstone's management of the estate. May be some monkey-doodling there. I never," he finished, "bothered with such details before. It may be that I'm too advanced in life to turn detective. But this case," he said, "this case has got me so Goddamned curious!"

They cheered him faintly.

"Besides," he said a little bitterly, "now that you two have robbed the Blake County jail of its one murderer, I've got to provide another one or be damned forever."

"Teacher," said Helene simply, "I never would of done it if I had of knew."

Jake was busily writing something at the desk. "Note for Dick," he said, "explaining everything, telling him to sit tight, say nothing, and hold rehearsal as usual until he hears from us."

Malone found his hat under the bed. "I'll bring my car around and drive you out to Maple Park."

After he had gone, Jake lifted the bottle from the dresser.

"Shame to waste this," he said.

They divided it with mathematical precision.

Jake tried to think of the word that meant Helene's beauty. Flawless was almost it, but not quite.

"Tell me," he said, "what does it all mean, anyway? Who are you, and who am I, and why are we here?"

"I'll tell you," she said dreamily, "when you tell me who did the murder."

"The hell with the murder. What does it all add up to?"

"It isn't real," she told him. "You're not here, and I'm not here. There is no such place as this room. Nobody's been murdered. Holly isn't being hunted by the police. Aunt Alex— For God's sake," she said, "hand me that drink and be done with it."

He handed the glass to her solemnly.

"Thanks."

"You're welcome."

She set the glass down on the dresser, empty.

"Nothing is real," she said very softly.

Her arms slid around his neck, her fingers crept along his shoulders. He felt smooth blue satin grow warm like skin under his hands.

The telephone rang, and Malone was ready with the ear.

"This much is certain," she said very thoughtfully, wrapping her coat around her, "if this keeps up, sooner or later one or the other of us is going to be the victim of a rape."

He looked at her for a long appreciative moment.

"Yes," he promised, "and if it's me, I won't struggle."

CHAPTER 15

"WHERE IS Holly?" Glen asked anxiously.

Jake looked at the young man across the gloomy Inglehart library and decided he hadn't been sleeping well. He was very pale and very tired.

"Don't you know?" Jake asked in a surprised voice.

"No. Of course not. I assumed all along that you knew."

"Well, well," said Malone, "quite a coincidence!"

Glen stared at them. "You mean you thought I planned her escape?"

"Didn't you?" Jake said mildly. "I could have sworn you pushed her down that laundry chute."

"Don't joke about this," Glen said in a desperate tone. "She may be dead. She might have fallen over the bluff. God only knows what's happened to her. I thought all along that you—"

"We did," Helene said suddenly. "She's hidden somewhere, perfectly safe and out of danger."

Glen looked relieved. "I thought so. I remembered your sliding down the laundry chute to see if you could do it, and when she popped down it like that, I thought that was what was up. That's why I led everybody down the wrong staircase afterward."

"It was a help, too," Jake told him.

"I'm glad," Glen said gratefully. "God, I couldn't stand thinking of her in jail. But I hate to have her run away like this. Maybe she's safe, but it isn't enough. I don't want people thinking she's a murderess. She's my own sister, my twin sister." He drew a long breath. "Maybe I've no business to ask questions. But has she run away with Dick Dayton? I like Dick. I think he's a swell guy. I wanted her to marry him, yes, in spite of Aunt Alex. It didn't matter about the money, really. Because I'd have seen that she got her share after Aunt Alex died anyway."

Helene looked at him sympathetically. "You look as though you'd been sleeping in your clothes."

"I have been," Glen said briefly. He hesitated a moment. "Look, Holly really didn't have a motive. She knew that I'd see to it she got her share of the estate after Aunt Alex died, whether she married Dick or not. So it couldn't have been Holly. And I think I know just what did happen."

"Hm?" said Malone inquiringly and noncommittally.

"It must have been done—the murder I mean—by some outsider. Someone who came in the house while we were away. That's what the phone call was for. I mean, someone wanted to get Parkins and me away from here. Someone who knew Nellie was away. I mean, they knew she was away and so they called up and pretended to be Holly. I'm getting this a little mixed up, I guess. But anyway, whoever it was came in while we were gone and stabbed Aunt Alex. That's how it happened."

"Let me get this straight," Malone said, "if I can. You believe that whoever telephoned you that night was imitating your sister's voice."

"That's it."

"Do you remember anything about the voice?"

"No. That is—it sounded like Holly's voice. Of course I'd

been asleep and just waked up. It sounded like Holly's voice and whoever it was said, 'This is Holly.' So of course I just assumed it was Holly. If I'd noticed—sort of subconsciously, I mean—that it didn't sound like Holly—I'd have assumed that it was because she'd been in an accident. See what I mean?"

"I see," said John J. Malone. "And then when you and Parkins had been lured away, this unknown person came in and murdered your aunt?"

"Yes. That's it."

"But," said Jake thoughtfully, "who the hell would want to murder your aunt? Pardon me, I didn't mean to put it just that way. But in any murder you've got to have four distinct elements. Murderer, murderee, method, and motive. Now we have a murderee in the person of your Aunt Alex; Blake County has named one murderer and we're looking for another; you've just outlined a possible method; but where," he said, "where in the name of Judas is the motive?"

"I don't know," Glen said thoughtfully. "But somebody must have wanted to murder Aunt Alex, or nobody would have."

Jake muttered rude words under his breath.

"What about this bird Featherstone?" Malone asked.

"Motive?"

"Maybe he's been embezzling your account," Malone said. "I'm sure as hell going to find out, anyway."

There was a short pause.

"He almost married Aunt Alex, years ago," Helene said. "I remember Mother telling me about it. Nobody knows what broke it off."

"Possible motive there too," Malone said.

There was a longer pause while everyone tried to imagine O. O. Feather-stone imitating Holly's voice over the wire, luring

Glen and Parkins away from the house with the accident story, climbing in the window of Alexandria Ingelhart's room, and murdering her. No one could.

"You forget," said John J. Malone, spilling ashes on his necktie. "Where was Holly while all this was going on?"

The silence was almost deafening.

"She's shielding somebody," said Glen helpfully. "She thinks someone she loves did it, and she's telling this insane and incredible story—Dayton, for instance, she loves him—"

"Dick was leading the band at the Blue Casino until after four in the morning," Jake reminded him.

Glen blinked at him. "Well, somebody. Maybe—Oh God, maybe she thinks *I* did it and she's trying to shield me."

"Well, did you?" Jake said nastily.

Glen ignored him. "If Holly hadn't gotten out of jail, I was going to confess to the murder."

"Glen," Helene began imploringly. "You don't really mean—"

"Why haven't I a motive too?" Glen went on. "Aunt Alex always held me down and I didn't have any money of my own and wouldn't have until she was dead. I was going to tell them I did it, and that would give Holly a chance to get away."

"You forget," Malone said kindly, "the police knew very well that at three o'clock you were in a car with the Parkinses, coming back from town."

Glen sighed.

"And where was Holly at three o'clock?" Helene asked.

No one answered.

Jake sat regarding Helene admiringly, thinking that what she had was not beauty, not loveliness, but a kind of perfection, and wondering what she was really like. He looked at them one by one: the short, red-faced Malone, his eyelids swollen, his

necktie creeping towards one ear; Glen, his olive skin unnat-
urally pale, his damp black hair rumpled; Helene, her brilliant
blue eyes expressionless in her marblelike face.

The room was terribly still. Something dark and cold crept
into Jake's brain. The aftermath of a hangover, he told himself angrily, but he knew it was not the hang-over. There was a
smell of death in the room, death and a premonition of horror
yet to come, of terror unspeakable and indescribable, of blood,
violence, and a world gone red and mad. Was it some inexpli-
cable communication? He didn't know, he didn't dare know.
But he did know that there would be tragedy and that it would
touch himself—that Somebody—he didn't know who—was going to die, horribly, hideously, and that he was going to watch
that person die, helplessly, that he was going to hear that person shrieking in the face of sudden death while the very sky ran
scarlet and flaming—

"Where the hell are all the matches in this house?" said Helene suddenly in the silence, and the spell was broken.

Before anyone could say another word, Parkins opened the
library door to admit the pessimistic Mr. Fleck.

Jasper Fleck was an unhappy man. Being familiar with Maple Park, it was his duty to assist the county authorities in this
painful matter. It was an unpleasant and embarrassing duty. He
had been chief of police of Maple Park for nearly thirty years,
and he'd never had any trouble like this before. It had been his
job to prevent any possible annoyance coming to the residents of
Maple Park, to protect them from irritations, and occasionally
to straighten out the little difficulties they would get themselves
into, in their impetuous way. He had a vague feeling in the back
of his mind that this little murder was just another of the impet-

uous things these Maple Park people would do occasionally, and that he ought to be able to smooth it over.

"I don't like this business," he said unhappily, after greeting them. "There haven't been no murders in Maple Park since that Filipino butler of the Bradshaws' carved up the cook, back in 'twenty-five, and that was different."

"None of us like it," Malone said briskly.

Jasper Fleck sighed heavily "It don't seem to me like she could of done it without she was out of her mind, which she certainty must have been from the way things seem to have happened out here. If it hadn't been for her getting out of jail that way, I'd say she hadn't done it."

Both Jake and Helene caught the reproachful look Malone gave them.

"Maybe she just didn't like the Blake County jail," Helene said.

"Well," said Jasper Fleck thoughtfully, "without it was a robbery—" He paused and scratched his eyebrow. "Without it was a robbery—we do have robberies in Maple Park even if we don't have murders."

"You've had one murder," Jake reminded him.

"Well," Fleck said again, "the window was open. Why should a window be open when it was that cold outside, without somebody wanted to get in it or get out of it? And there wasn't nobody in the house that wanted to get out of the window, so it stands to reason somebody might of wanted to get in the house, and who would of wanted to get in without it was because of a robbery?"

It was wonderful!

"And of course," said Helene, "Aunt Alex, a helpless invalid, was such a threat to the safety and well-being of this alleged burglar that she had to be killed."

Mr. Fleck gulped.

"To say nothing of the fact that nothing was taken."

"I only meant," said Jasper Fleck defensively, "that's the way it could of happened if it had of been a robbery." He emitted a tomblike sigh. "But that isn't what I came here for. It's you, Miss Brand. They told me next door you might be over here."

"What have I done now?" Helene asked.

"There have been some complaints about your driving. Mrs. Ridgeway next door—she didn't like your driving across her lawn."

"I skidded," said Helene briefly, "on the ice. Since I was coming here anyway, I kept right on going. Mrs. Ridgeway is an old fuddyduddy."

"But you weren't driving your car last night," Glen said.

"It wasn't last night," Mr. Fleck said, "it was night before last. The night of the murder." He looked at Helene unhappily "If you go on doing things like that, Miss Brand, someday I'm going to have to arrest you."

"I'll be good," Helene promised in an affectionate tone. "And I'll square things with Mrs. Ridgeway."

Mr. Fleck looked relieved. He reached for his hat. "It's a good thing none of you had anything to do with Miss Holly getting away last night. Hyme Mendel's plenty sore. He said—" He paused, evidently concluded Hyme Mendel's words were not appropriate to the Inglehart library, said good morning to them all and went away.

"Well," said Helene after a while, "we can all prove our innocence. Jake and I were right here and we helped him look for her. You, Malone, were parked in Jake's room at the hotel. Dick was leading his band."

"Just the same," Malone growled, "you've put me in a hell of a spot. And everybody in this damned case is lying." He glared at Helene and Glen. "You two. If you want to help Holly, you'd better come clean."

Jake hardly heard him. He was thinking over what Jasper Fleck had said.

But Malone's next words brought him back to earth.

"For one thing," Malone was saying, "I want to know just what Parkins meant when he spoke of the wrong that had been done his daughter. And I have a hunch you know what it is."

Helene and Glen looked at each other. Then Helene rose slowly and deliberately, walked to the window, looked out for a moment, walked back again.

"He's right, Glen," she said. "He's got to be told. And I'm going to tell him myself."

CHAPTER 16

"There isn't so much to it, really," Helene said slowly, "and there isn't any real reason why it shouldn't be told. Except for Glen."

"Forget that stuff," Glen said almost savagely. "No one has to protect me." He turned to Malone. "Maybelle was brought up here. We all played together as kids. Maybelle and I grew up and had a love affair and Aunt Alex kicked her out of the house. That's all there is to the story."

"Glen," Helene said. "Glen, don't."

"Shut up, Helene. I've been paying for her apartment in Rogers Park. I couldn't marry her because Aunt Alex would have tossed me out on my ear. If it hadn't been for Aunt Alex, I would have married her."

Helene shrugged her shoulders in the pause that followed. "Well Glen, it's your funeral."

"So you did have a motive for murdering your aunt," Malone said mildly. "Well, well. Live and learn."

"Are you going to marry her now?" Jake asked.

"My God! Is this any time to think of things like that? I don't know. I haven't had time to think. I've never really known what I wanted to do about it. Even when I knew Aunt Alex was going to die, I didn't look that far ahead."

"What do you mean?" Malone asked a little stupidly.

"Aunt Alex didn't have long to live. Dr. Neville—her doctor—told us so. Told Holly and me, and old Featherstone. I don't know if anyone else knew it."

"Why, in the name of all that's holy," Malone said, "hasn't someone mentioned this before?"

"I don't know. I guess nobody thought it was important."

"Important!" For a moment Malone talked briefly and explicitly to God.

"If she was going to die anyway," Jake said, "what was the use of murdering her?"

"But only Glen and Holly and Featherstone and the doctor knew it," Helene reminded him.

"What's the doctor's address?" Malone asked.

Glen told him; he wrote it down.

"Someone who didn't know she hadn't long to live," Jake mused. "Glen, we come back again to your theory of an outsider."

"Or," Malone said, "there was some reason why she had to die on that particular night."

"What reason?" Glen asked.

"Because she was going to change her will the next day," Malone told him. He walked to the door, opened it, and bawled loudly for Nellie. She appeared at the end of the hall.

"Mrs. Parkins. Did you tell anyone that Miss Inglehart planned to change her will?"

"No, sir."

"Not anyone?"

"Not even Parkins, Mr. Malone."

Malone banged the door and came back into the library. "I've no doubt Featherstone will tell me the same thing." He paused to mop his face. "That's a break for you, Glen."

"For *me?*"

"If you'd known she was going to change her will you might have thought she planned to disinherit you, and murdered her yourself."

"But why should she disinherit *me?*" Glen asked wildly.

"Maybelle Parkins."

Helene frowned. "If Aunt Alex planned to disinherit Glen because of Maybelle Parkins, why didn't she do it months ago instead of waiting all this time?"

"Maybe she didn't like to make quick decisions," Jake said.

Helene snorted rudely.

Malone looked at his watch. "I still have to visit Featherstone's office and talk to that doctor," he announced, "and thanks to our having wasted the morning sleeping, it's three o'clock."

Again there was something Jake wanted to remember. Oh well, it would come to him. He sighed. "We always come back to one question," he said. "Where was Holly at three o'clock?"

No one answered.

Malone put his hat on a little crookedly. "I have a feeling," he said, "this is a murder of motive, not of method. Once I find the motive for it, the method will be clear." He brushed the ashes off his vest. "Jake, you and Helene will have to talk to my client. You know where she is. Find out if she knew her aunt planned to change her will. Ask her everything you can think of about that night. And for the love of God remember what she tells you, so you can tell me tonight." He turned to Glen. "You had better stay right here and go on convincing the police that you don't know how your sister got away from them. And you, Helene, if you have any other clothes, you'd better put them on."

He was gone before Helene could make an appropriate answer.

She rose a little wearily. "Come on, Jake. We'll go the back way, it's shorter."

They said good-by to Glen, reminded him to keep his chin up, and went out the delivery entrance.

They stepped out into the cold wind and walked along the driveway to where it hid itself in a grove of trees. There they paused for a moment and looked over the expanse of snow that lay between the old house and the lake.

"Nothing to do with the case, but it *is* a nice backyard," Jake remarked.

He was seeing it again as he had seen it through Alexandria Inglehart's window, standing beside Alexandria Inglehart's withered old body. An acre or so of snow-covered ground, spotted with clumps of great dark trees, blotched and bumpy and discolored with what were undoubtedly shrubs and bushes in the summer. Now it was desolation.

He pointed to a low, odd-shaped building near the cliff's edge.

"That?" Helene said. "That's the old summerhouse. Holly's grandfather built it. I don't know how long it's been since it was used. When we were kids, we used to pretend it was haunted. Aunt Alex always kept it locked, never would let any of us go near it. There's furniture there, of a sort. Want to take a look?"

"Sure."

They plowed through knee-deep snow to the lake shore. The gently sloping ground suddenly became a cliff that hung over the gray and wind-lashed water. There was a sheer drop, studded with jagged rocks, and below, great round boulders, sharp gray stones with cruelly pointed edges, immense blocks of ice tossed there by the waves. The water, stormy and seething and filled with cakes of dirty ice, beat continually against the rocks, breaking over them in gusts of livid foam.

"Nice place for a fall," Jake reflected.

"It isn't so bad in the summertime."

"It's just as far down in the summertime," he said angrily. "Didn't anyone ever think of putting a railing here?"

Helene shook her head. "Someone did fall over here once, years ago. But no one else ever did, so people figured it wasn't really dangerous."

A few wind-twisted trees clung to the edge of the cliff; beyond them the deserted and dreary summerhouse loomed against the snow. It was a dark brown building, ugly and forbidding. They wiped the snow from a window and peered inside.

"Jake! Someone's been living here!"

"You're nuts!"

"What's that got to do with it? Look for yourself!"

He stared in through the window. As his eyes became used to the semi-darkness, he could dimly see chairs and a table, a disordered couch covered with quilts and blankets. There were dishes on the table and the remains of a meal, half a loaf of bread, a hunk of butter on a chipped saucer, a half-empty package of cigarettes.

"By God, someone *is* living here," Jake said.

He looked around. "No footprints, though."

"You forget it snowed again last night," she told him acidly, "or didn't you notice?"

"Where was I last night? Oh yes, I guess I didn't notice."

"Jake, what are we going to do?"

"Tell the police."

"Hyme Mendel is the police. Nuts to him."

"You've got to tell somebody," he said.

"Jake, look." She caught his arm. "There's the house, up there. And that window—the big one—looking this way—"

"A pretty picture, but what of it?"

"It's the window where Aunt Alex was sitting."

"So it's not a pretty picture, and still what of it?"

"Whoever is living in the summerhouse could see her. If he happened to be looking that way—"

"By God, you *are* nuts!"

"Besides, who would be living in the Inglehart summerhouse? Jake, it's the unknown element—the unknown person. It's—"

"It's probably a tramp, taking advantage of a warm place to sleep."

"Tramps don't smoke Virginia Grays."

Jake was silent. He too had noticed the cigarette package.

"Besides," she said again, "whoever is living here could have seen Glen and Parkins go away, and gone into the house and murdered Aunt Alex. He could even have made the phone call that lured them away."

Jake only stared at her.

"We've got to watch the summerhouse," she said firmly.

He swore indignantly. "Where do we watch from? Camped out here in the snow, like a couple of Eskimos? Maybe you'd like me to build you an igloo."

"We can see the summerhouse from our garage," she told him.

"I admit this is important," he told her, "but seeing Holly is important, too."

"That's true." She looked at her watch. "And I thought we'd pay a visit to Maybelle Parkins. She seems to be the forgotten woman in this case." She sighed and hummed a line of *I Wish That You Were Twins*.

"Butch!" she said suddenly.

"What about him?"

"We'll set him to watch the summerhouse until we can do it ourselves. And until we can tell Malone about it. He'll know what to do. Come on."

They started toward the old stone gate.

"I think," she said slowly, "I think we've found something. Possibly Aunt Alex's murderer. Or a witness to her murder." She was silent for a few steps. "I wonder. I wonder if he saw—Holly."

CHAPTER 17

"I HAVEN'T seen Maybelle since she was about fifteen," said Helene thoughtfully, parking the big car in front of an apartment building in Rogers Park. "I remember her as a thinnish child with the kind of blonde hair that turns dark early."

"So?" Jake said, looking at her admiringly. The blue pajamas and fur coat had been replaced by something expensive and beautiful of tweed and fur. He wondered what kind of negligees she wore.

"So the hair will be blondined, the brassy kind. She will have much make-up on, with the wrong kind of lipstick. Her dress will be the latest model, but cost four-ninety-eight, and it will have perspiration stains. Her neck will be dirty. And she will have run-over heels."

The young woman who opened the door answered Helene's description perfectly except for one detail. She wore flat-footed bedroom slippers.

"Well, what do you want?" she said suspiciously.

"You're Miss Parkins?" Jake asked.

"That's me. You might as well trot right along, because whatever you're selling, I don't want to buy it." Then she recognized Helene. "Oh, Miss Brand. I hardly knew you."

"So many people don't," Helene murmured.

She showed them into a small, garish, and amazingly disordered one-room apartment.

"I'm frightfully sorry everything is in such a mess. I simply didn't dream anyone would be coming to see me."

"Perfectly all right," Helene smiled at her brightly. "This is such a cozy little place."

"I like it," Maybelle said, beaming.

She offered them chairs, bright-colored ash trays made in the shape of peculiar little birds, and a grade of whisky that set the fillings in Jake's teeth to rattling.

"I guess you've come to talk about the murder. Isn't it simply awful? Poor Glen is so upset about it." She patted her hair. "I've been saving all the newspaper clippings and putting them in a scrapbook."

She found the scrapbook under a pile of gaudy magazines.

"I've been terribly excited about it. It's the first thing like this I've ever been, well, what you might call closely connected with." She smiled coyly and opened the scrapbook.

Every clipping was there—from the discovery of the body of Alexandria Inglehart, to the disappearance of Holly Dayton. Jake felt a little ill.

"I'm so glad Holly escaped," she rattled on. "That Mr. Dayton must feel so relieved. To think," she said wide-eyed, "to think that I used to listen to him night after night on the radio, and simply worship him, and now Glen's sister is married to him."

"My," said Helene, "that makes you practically his sister-in-law."

Maybelle stared at her.

"Do you really love Glen?" Helene asked theatrically.

Maybelle began sniffing artistically into a lipstick-stained handkerchief. "I'd die for him. I'd do anything for him. There never could be another man in my life. Never."

Jake decided Maybelle had been reading a very low grade of fiction.

"When you're married—" Helene began.

"Oh no. It's impossible." Maybelle began to sniff again.

"Why?" Helene asked. "Aunt Alex couldn't raise any objection now."

"That isn't it. Glen doesn't love me." The tears threatened to become a flood. "I've done everything for him. I was going to take a course in beauty culture and have a little shop of my own someday, and I gave it up just to keep up this little home so that he could come here whenever he wanted to, and I've quarreled with my father about him, and given up everything for him."

She forgot to mention the best years of her life, Jake thought.

She consoled herself a little with the whisky bottle.

"Do you remember the night of the murder?" Jake asked suddenly.

"Remember it! Oh, I'll never forget it. It was so awful. Really it was. Nellie was here all evening and she was going to spend the night, and about midnight, no I guess it was later, because Glen said the streets were dreadful coming in from Maple Park, and they all thought Holly had been hurt in an accident and we were all so terribly upset, and Glen was just like a ghost, and then they all went on down to the hospital and left me here all alone to worry." She paused for breath. "And then nobody thought to phone and tell me what had happened and I didn't find out anything about it until I went to the store in the morning and saw a paper."

She said it as though she had been memorizing it.

"Did you know Miss Inglehart had left you a thousand dollars?" Jake asked.

Maybelle's round chin dropped. "She *did!*"

Jake nodded.

"How wonderful! I mean—I can't believe it!"

She was silent, staring at them. It seemed to Jake that she was already planning the spending of it.

But Maybelle Parkins had no information that would help them. Jake managed to get them away from her apartment before she could offer them another drink of the whisky.

"Maybelle should go to better movies than she does," Helene said as they drove away.

"She could have imitated Holly's voice over the phone," Jake said thoughtfully. "She knew Holly all her life. And then gone out to the house and murdered the old woman while Glen and the Parkinses were gone."

"Why?"

"For a thousand dollars," Jake said. "I bet that dame would murder twenty people for a thousand dollars."

"I'll raise it to forty. But she didn't know about the thousand dollars."

"She says she didn't," Jake said sourly.

"Nice trusting nature," Helene murmured.

"Besides, the old woman stood in the way of her marrying Glen."

"Can you really see Glen marrying that floozie?" Helene asked.

"No. But he might have thought he ought to."

"All right," Helene said. "So Maybelle lured Glen and the Parkinses away from the house and nipped out to Maple Park and stabbed Aunt Alex, and nipped back again. But where was Holly while she was doing it?"

Jake groaned. "We'll ask Holly when we see her. Maybe she'll remember something after a good night's sleep." He considered for a moment. "Maybelle would never have thought of anything so elaborate."

"All right. Pa Parkins thought of it. Maybe Nellie Parkins."

"Nellie Parkins looks just a bit on the sinister side," Jake observed. "She'd make a damned promising prospect for the murderer. Except that she couldn't have done it."

"She's a type that could commit a murder without batting an eyelash," Helene said, "cold-bloodedly and with deliberation. And without changing the expression on her face. But she never would let the blame fall on Holly."

"The same goes for Pa Parkins."

"Jake, who murdered Aunt Alex?"

Jake shook his head wearily. "If this keeps up, I'll begin to believe she never was murdered. Or that I did it myself."

CHAPTER 18

THEY FOUND Madam Fraser engaged in teaching Holly the intricacies of a new knitting stitch.

"Oh, hello," the gray-haired woman said as they came in the door. Then to Holly, "No, dearie, no. You wind the yarn around twice, and then—"

"Show me too," Helene said.

There was a brief discussion of the pattern, the eventual effect, and the kind of yarn to use. Jake thought it gave a pleasantly cozy touch to the murder.

"What's been happening?" Holly said, after Mrs. Fraser had gone. "For heaven's sake, what's been happening?"

"Everyone is looking for you," Jake told her. "Hyme Mendel is losing his mind. You've been reported seen in Omaha, Nebraska, Lansing, Michigan, and the ladies' room of the Boston Store. In Bloomington they held six red-haired women in jail all morning on the theory that one of them might be the missing murderess from Maple Park."

"Why doesn't Dick come to see me?"

"It wouldn't do," Helene said. "Everybody recognizes him from his pictures. We can come here without being watched."

"You see," said Jake, "they probably figure that Dick will go to see you and that he'll lead the police to where you are."

Holly stood up suddenly and walked to the window. "I keep being afraid that—"

"That what?" Helene asked.

"That he believes I did it and he'd just rather not—well, rather not."

"Don't be a dope," said Jake magnificently. "In the first place, he's convinced you didn't do it. In the second place, he wouldn't care if you'd murdered fifty aunts, one after another. And once you're cleared of this ridiculous charge—"

"Is it a ridiculous charge?" Holly said slowly.

"Look here," said Helene, "look here. There's a lot of things you can do and not remember about, but believe me, anyone who murdered Aunt Alex would never forget it."

"But," said Holly, "but don't you see—"

"Listen to me," Jake said sternly, "there's only two possibilities. Either you killed her, or you didn't. I subscribe to the latter theory. It's not important, but in case I'm right, it would be nice to prove it."

She almost smiled.

"There seems so damn little motive for this thing," he said. "You apparently have a motive, but we know that what looks like a cause for murder to the eye of Hyme Mendel really wasn't anything of the kind."

He paused and grinned at her. "As Glen put it, somebody must have wanted to murder Aunt Alex, or nobody would have. Or more explicitly, before you can murder anybody with a Florentine paper knife, you've got to murder him in your mind, with your desire to murder him."

"Especially," Helene said slowly, "in a crime as obviously premeditated as this one."

"It was premeditated," said Holly suddenly. "It must have been. But if it was—" she paused, thought a moment. "You'd think anyone who came up to that room to—to do what was done—would have brought some kind of weapon along unless—well, unless whoever it was knew that the paper knife was there."

"Knew that it was there, and that it was deadly enough to be used as a weapon," Jake said excitedly. "By God, nobody has thought of that before."

"You see, Holly," Helene said, "you can help."

"Who would have known about the paper knife?" Jake asked.

"I would. Glen would. The Parkinses would."

"Maybelle?"

"I suppose so. Yes, she would."

"Anyone else? Featherstone?"

"Possibly. No one else."

Jake sighed. "Six people. Of them, three are out, unless they got together and connived at this. I mean Glen and the Parkinses. And I can't see them conspiring, somehow."

"Neither can I," said Helene.

"But according to all their stories, they were riding through the streets of Chicago at the time Aunt Alex met her Maker. And I'd be willing to bet Mr. O. O. Featherstone will turn out to have an ironclad alibi."

"We keep getting back," Helene said, "to the fact that there must be someone we don't know about involved in this "

"But who?" Holly asked.

"If we knew who, we would answer a lot of questions," Jake said. "Someone who had a motive to murder Alexandria Inglehart. Someone who knew that she would have a paper knife on her table, a paper knife that would stab an old woman to death."

Holly shook her head. "It isn't possible."

"But there *is* someone else involved in this," Helene said. "We know there is." She told Holly of the inhabited summerhouse.

Holly listened round-eyed. "Who could it be?"

"That's what we're going to find out."

Jake remembered something. "Did you know your Aunt Alex planned to change her will?"

Holly nodded slowly.

"You did!" Helene exclaimed.

"I overheard it. I'd just come back to the house and I sneaked in, because I was late. I heard Nellie telephone to Mr. Featherstone. I don't know why I didn't think more about it at the time. I guess I was too excited about running away with Dick to think of anything."

"Damn it," Jake exploded, "everything we learn gets you deeper into this."

"Did you know your Aunt Alex didn't have long to live?" Helene asked.

Again Holly nodded. "Dr. Neville told me."

They talked through dinner and through the evening. But when Jake and Helene prepared to go, they had learned nothing more about the murder of Alexandria Inglehart.

Holly had one last idea. "Why was the window opened?"

"Probably the murder was committed by a fresh-air fiend," Helene said, wrapping her furs around her shoulders. "Which explains the whole thing." She patted Holly's shoulder. "We'll try to figure a way to smuggle Dick in to see you."

Holly's eyes glowed. "All this will be over soon, won't it? I mean, it's got to be over. And then Dick and I will be together and there won't be anything to separate us. Not anything. Ever."

"I'm going home and help watch the summerhouse," Helene said, down at the car. "And you?"

"I'd come with you. But I want to see Dick, and talk to Malone."

They found a corner drugstore where Jake phoned Malone's apartment and learned that the lawyer was waiting for him at the hotel.

"If you didn't have the summerhouse on your mind," he began.

"I do," Helene told him. "I'll drop you off at the hotel, and then I'm going home."

He sighed. "Eventually—"

"Eventually," she said.

He kissed her warmly in front of the hotel, to the delight of the doorman, bought a paper in the lobby, tucked it under his arm, and went upstairs.

John J. Malone was sitting on the bed waiting for him, surrounded by a squirrel's nest of papers, notes, clothing, and bottles.

"No luck with Featherstone," he reported, "the Inglehart affairs are in order down to the last ninety-eight cents."

"Maybe he murdered her for thwarted love," Jake said, thinking of Helene. "How long have you been waiting here?"

"Since dinnertime. I took a nap."

"What did Dr. Neville tell you?" Jake asked, spreading open the newspaper he had bought.

"Nothing that we don't know already."

Jake didn't hear him. "My God! Malone!"

"What?"

"Look!" He fairly hurled the paper at the lawyer.

Malone looked and turned pale.

HOLLY'S HUSBAND ALSO VANISHES

ORCHESTRA LEADER DISAPPEARS AFTER

BRIDE'S JAILBREAK

Jake was at the telephone. When he set it down a minute later, his face was very white.

"He hasn't been seen since about noon. He left the hotel and just vanished. Didn't show up for rehearsal. Hasn't shown up since. My God, Malone—what's happened to him?"

CHAPTER 19

"THERE ISN'T anything you can do," Malone kept repeating. "You'll only be in the way. There isn't anything you can do." He kept saying it over and over like a cracked phonograph record.

"The hell there isn't," said Jake, tying his shoelace.

"You need sleep."

"I had some last night," Jake said. "That ought to hold me for a while." He lit a cigarette, puffed at it nervously "Naturally they figure Holly's escape and Dick's disappearance are part of the same thing. So now they're looking for the pair of them. A fine mess."

"What do you mean?" asked Malone, watching the tall man closely.

"Because they're looking for an escaping couple and not for two separate individuals, which makes everything very squirrelly. The chances of their running down Holly are subsequently lessened. That was almost zero anyway. But their chances of finding Dick are also just that much less. Oh hell."

"Well, of course," Malone said, "if you'd been satisfied to let well enough alone—"

"I couldn't foresee this, could I?" He began combing his hair nervously.

"It looks to me as though you couldn't foresee anything," Malone said severely. "What do you think you're going to do?"

"I'm going out and find Dick."

"Where?"

"Wherever he is, you fat fool."

"And just where," Malone asked icily, "do you intend to look?"

"I'll start at the *Tribune* Lost and Found bureau," Jake said nastily.

"You don't know where he's gone," the lawyer continued, "you haven't the faintest idea where he might go, or what might have happened to him. There isn't anything you can do."

"I can try to trace him. I can ask questions at the desk and—"

"You won't find anybody to question, at this hour of the night. Try to get some sleep."

"Hell, no. I'm going out and look for Dick."

Malone looked at him thoughtfully. The tall man was swaying on his feet, his gray eyes were red-rimmed and swollen.

"Stop arguing and get into that bed."

"No. Get out of my way—"

Malone collapsed him with one nicely calculated punch. With the help of a bellhop he tucked him into bed and went away, locking the door behind him and leaving the key at the desk downstairs, with instructions to call Mr. Justus and let him out at eight in the morning.

It was nearly eight when he returned, from a night spent listening to police reports, following the search for Dick and Holly. He found Jake still sleeping, brought him to a sudden and profane awakening with a splash of icy water.

"Dick?"

"No news."

Jake dressed hurriedly, muttering to himself. "Among other things, what happened to the band last night?"

"That skinny clarinet player handled it."

"Oh, Steve. I guess that's all right."

"They tell me the Casino was packed."

"It would be. Do you think Dick is dead?"

"No. Why would anyone—"

"I don't know."

"He maybe passed out in the back room of a bar somewhere," said Malone.

"Not Dick."

"People do. I remember once when you disappeared for five days, and—"

"Yes, but not Dick."

"But where the hell could he have gone?"

"That's what I asked you," Jake said irritably, tying his tie. He pulled on his hat with a vicious jerk. "Hoist your fat bucket out of that chair and come on."

"Someone may have come here to see him," said Malone thoughtfully. "He may have left the hotel with someone. He may have had telephone calls."

The girl who had been on the switchboard was taking the day off, and was home, sleeping. She answered Jake's telephone call in a drowsy and indignant voice.

"You'd be cross too, Mr. Justus, if someone got you out of bed at this time in the morning. Yes, Mr. Dayton had a telephone call in the early afternoon. Just one. It was around one o'clock. I'm sure of it because I always notice the calls that come for him."

"You didn't notice what was said, did you?"

"I have plenty of other things to do besides listening in on Mr. Dayton's phone conversations."

"All right, all right. And then what?"

"Then he tried to get in touch with you."

"You're sure?"

"Yes, you. He spent about half an hour calling every place he thought you might be. And I must say, Mr. Justus—"

"Leave my personal habits out of this," said Jake hastily. "What then?"

"Then he came downstairs and left a message with Al at the desk, and went out. That's all I know."

"Thanks, sister," said Jake. "You've been a help. Go back to bed."

"One phone call. Might have been anything," Malone said.

Al, the desk clerk, was just coming on duty. He remembered that Dick had seen no visitors, had come downstairs some time after one o'clock, and left a message at the desk.

"It was for you, Mr. Justus. Just that if you phoned or came in, you were to wait, because he was coming back in a couple of hours. He said he wanted to see you as soon as he could, because it was very important."

Jake groaned. "But he didn't come back, Malone. He was trying to locate me. He tried to find me, and I wasn't around, and he went off somewhere on his own. And he didn't come back. He expected to come back, and he didn't."

"You couldn't help it," Malone told him.

"That doesn't make me feel any better." He lit a cigarette, took one puff, stamped it out under his heel. "We'll try the doorman."

The doorman remembered that Mr. Dayton had called a taxi

and told the driver to take him to Ricketts. Jake breathed a sigh of relief.

"That's a start, anyway. They'll remember him at Ricketts, and someone may remember who he came in with, or if he met someone there."

"We hope!" said Malone soulfully.

They drove to Ricketts.

"Mr. Dayton?" said the bartender thoughtfully. He stood polishing the bar for a moment. "Yes, he was in yesterday afternoon. Just a little before two, it was. He looked pretty rocky, too. Like it had been a big night, if you know what I mean. And he acted like he had something on his mind, too. No wonder, with his wife in all that trouble. Not friendly and cheerful like he usually is. Couldn't blame him, either. Had two beers."

"Beer," said Jake shuddering, "on the hang-over he must have had!"

"That's right, two beers. He sat here about half an hour and kept looking at his watch all the time. Then he called a taxi and left."

Jake swore.

"I could probably find you the driver," the bartender added helpfully. "He hangs around here most of the time."

"I could kiss you!" said Jake. "Find him!"

An errand boy was dispatched to scour the neighborhood. After what seemed endless moments of waiting, he returned with the taxi driver, who had been breakfasting in Thompson's next door.

The driver remembered picking Dick Dayton up at Ricketts a little after two.

"He told me to drive him around until three o'clock."

"Three o'clock?" said Jake suddenly.

"Yes, that's right. He said to drive around until three and then let him out at the northwest end of the Michigan Avenue Bridge. I drove up Michigan to Lincoln Park, down State to Schiller, over Schiller to the Drive, along the Drive to Oak, turned east, and—"

"Never mind the guide to Chicago," said Jake hastily. "Tell me where you ended up."

"At the bridge, like he told me. Got there at three o'clock, right on the nose. When you're doing this all day, you get so you can estimate just where you can drive in how long. He got out at the bridge, right by the Wrigley Building, and tipped me fifty cents. Last I saw of him he was standing there at the end of the bridge, looking up and down the street like he was waiting for somebody. That was right at three o'clock."

There the trail ended. There was no one near the bridge who might have remembered seeing him, no newsstand boy, no doorman, no one. Only people passing there by the hundreds, few, if any, noticing the tall blond young man, fewer still recognizing Dick Dayton. And even those who had recognized him could never be found now, and even if they could be found, they would not know what had happened to Dick Dayton after he disappeared from the northwest end of the Michigan Avenue Bridge.

They gave up the trail and settled down to the obvious things. In a few hours the hospitals had been covered, the police stations and the morgue were ruled out, every associate of Dick's had been investigated, and still no one knew where he was. The newspapers went insane, the *American* printed Dick's handsome face in the second largest picture ever seen on its front page, the *Times* gave its cover to the words: "Where Are Dick and Bride?" The *News* abandoned itself to: "Nation

Hunts Dick and Holly." And Jake and Malone retired to Jake's room to confer.

Jake sat thinking for a few minutes. "He went wandering off by himself and got drunk and hasn't sobered up yet, or he had an attack of amnesia, or he got into a dive and somebody rolled him. Only all that is out because Dick never goes off on a drunk like that. Or he disregarded my orders and went looking for Holly. But that doesn't account for the telephone call."

"Or for his going to meet somebody at the Michigan Avenue Bridge," Malone said, adding, "of all places."

"At three o'clock," Jake said. "That three o'clock business keeps on repeating itself like the chorus of a lousy song." He thought of a question he had meant to ask Malone. If he had asked it, the Inglehart murder might have been settled a day sooner, and at least one life might have been saved. But his mind was too full of Dick. "Malone, where is he?"

"Don't ask me," Malone said.

"Somebody wanted to lure him away," Jake said.

"Somebody did lure him away," Malone corrected him.

"But why?"

"There aren't any whys in this Goddamned case," said Malone peevishly.

"All right then, *who?*"

Just then the phone rang. It was Helene.

"Yes. I've read the papers," she said. "I'm downstairs. Get on your horse and come down and meet me. I'll be in the bar, on the third stool from the left as you go in. If you can't find me, I'm the one in black with the red rose in her hair."

She hung up before he could offer other suggestions.

CHAPTER 20

As THEY walked into the bar they saw her, gazing at the bartender with an air of utter absorption. She wore black, a deep, rich, glossy black, tailored and close-fitting on her long, slender body. Furs hung carelessly over her shoulders. Her delicate profile showed, exquisitely pale, against the black of her wide felt hat.

Jake paused for a moment and forgot his troubles, and thought he had never seen anyone so perfectly patrician, so completely the colonel's lady.

"You've got to get more spin to it," the bartender was saying.

He gave a sudden whisk to a glass of beer so that it spun down the length of the bar and stopped smartly in front of a plumpish customer.

Helene watched carefully, nodded, and repeated his procedure with the glass of beer he handed her. It spun the length of the polished bar and crashed noisily on the floor.

"Too far," she murmured abstractedly.

"You don't have the control," the bartender told her.

Jake and Malone stopped to watch, fascinated.

The bartender drew her another glass. This skidded down

the bar, ricocheted against an ash tray and slid neatly into the lap of the plumpish customer.

"Sorry," said Helene.

The plumpish customer rose, bowed. "I apologize," he muttered. "Should have ducked."

"Perhaps," said the bartender, "perhaps you should practice with empty glasses. Miss Brand."

She shook her head. "They don't spin right. Draw me a couple more."

Jake and Malone decided it was time to join her.

"Beer?" asked Malone.

She nodded. "For breakfast."

"Oh, I see. Beer for breakfast."

"That's it. You see, sometimes I like beer for breakfast and then again other times I like beer for breakfast, and still other times I just like—"

"Beer for breakfast. Now me, sometimes, I like breakfast for breakfast, and sometimes I like breakfast for breakfast, and—"

"Beer is fun for breakfast," Helene reflected, "but it's more fun to throw it than to drink it."

She spun another glass perilously down the bar and by some miracle it stopped on the target. The customers cheered.

"By God," said Jake explosively, "Dick is missing, maybe kidnaped, maybe dead, and here you two idiots go on babbling about beer for breakfast."

"I'd rather babble about beer than cry into it," observed Helene. The last glass of beer overturned ignominiously halfway down the bar. "Time to quit." She gathered her furs about her shoulders and paraded regally to a secluded booth. They followed her, the waiter a few lengths behind.

"Beer," said Helene. "Rye," said Malone. "Coffee," said Jake. "What the hell?" said Helene.

"I can't drink," he told her, "I don't feel like it."

She shrugged her shoulders. "Well, what about it Malone? Is he strayed, kidnaped, or just dead?"

"Helene, for Christ's sake," Jake said.

She lit a cigarette and looked at him without expression. "I don't suppose you remember all the times you've interviewed people in a spot like this, and the things you used to think about them when they went off into spins this way, and how you used to swear that if it ever happened to you, you'd keep remembering that nothing could be done about it, and it was just as easy as not to hang on to your nerve."

"How did you know I used to think that?" asked Jake with his first grin that day.

She shrugged her shoulders again.

There was a long silence.

"Perhaps," Helene said at last, "we could borrow a checkerboard from the bartender."

"Oh God," said Jake suddenly. "Oh God, it's the sitting here and doing nothing, and knowing there's nothing to do but sit and wait for news, and wonder if he's alive or dead!"

Helene looked at him coldly. "When you get through having your last kitten, let us know."

"Stop picking on him," Malone said.

"What do *you* think happened?" she asked.

"I don't think—"

"He's been kidnaped," Jake said suddenly. He told Helene what they had already learned.

"But who'd want to kidnap Dick Dayton?"

No one answered.

"Did Dick ever just wander off by himself and get lost? Did he ever lose his memory?"

Jake muttered impolite words.

"He's been under a terrific strain," Malone said slowly.

"That doesn't explain the phone call. Or why he was standing on the corner of the Michigan Avenue Bridge at three o'clock in the afternoon," Jake said.

"He was waiting for someone," Helene said.

"Who?"

"Maybe he thought he was waiting for someone and he was really waiting for someone else."

"It's your inescapable logic," Malone said. "That's what I really love you for."

"I mean, someone called and pretended to be you, for instance, and he went there expecting to meet you and someone else carried him off."

"I wouldn't exactly make an appointment with him at the end of the Michigan Avenue Bridge, would I?" Malone said scornfully.

"Why ask me? Where do you meet people, Malone? I'd love to know. You meet so many people."

"Do you really want to know how to meet people?"

"How to meet people and make friends."

"Try breaking a fifty-dollar bill at a bar," Malone told her. "To get back to Dick Dayton—"

"Well, this unknown might have pretended to be somebody who would meet him at a place like that."

"Your unknown could hardly kidnap Dick right in the middle of the crowds that would be passing the bridge at that hour in the afternoon," Jake said. "But outside of that—"

"Maybe he was drugged," Malone said wearily.

"Who drug him and where to?" Helene asked.

Jake audibly wished them both in hell.

The bartender brought another round.

"Gosh, Mr. Justus, I hope Mr. Dayton will turn up all right. Wha'd'ya suppose could have happened to him?"

"I don't know," Jake said.

"Some of the band boys were in here around dinnertime, and they sure were upset about it. And he hadn't been missing so long then, either. Gosh, I hope nothing's happened to him."

"So do I," Jake said.

"Funny thing," said the bartender, wiping the table, "a fella phoned him from in here yesterday."

"Huh?"

"Yeah. Fancy-looking guy in an iron hat and yellow gloves. Hung around here quite a little while. Called Dayton from the phone behind the bar."

"What did he say?" Jake asked with no apparent interest.

"I dunno. I just heard him ask for Dick Dayton. I wasn't paying much attention. All I heard was when he hung up he said, 'I'll be looking for you.' Just that. 'I'll be looking for you.'"

Further inquiries elicited the information that the little man had worn a Chesterfield overcoat, carried a Malacca cane, and had a trim little mustache. That was all the bartender knew.

"Probably nothing important. Just forget it," Jake advised.

The bartender nodded. "Well, I hope he'll turn up all right." He went away.

"I've always said," Helene remarked, "if you really want to know anything, ask a taxi driver or a bartender."

"We know what the guy looked like," Jake said, "but who is he?"

No one had any suggestions.

"It's possible, you know," Malone offered, "that this hasn't anything to do with the Inglehart murder."

"Somebody who wanted to kidnap Dick and picked this time to do it," said Jake slowly."But who? He doesn't make that much money."

"Maybe somebody who doesn't like his orchestra," said Helene, and then suddenly, "Oh God, I forgot. There's another mysterious stranger still unaccounted for."

"What are you talking about?" Malone asked.

"The man in the summerhouse. The tramp who can't be a tramp. Didn't Jake tell you?"

"I didn't," Jake said. "I intended to tell Malone about it as soon as I saw him. Then everything went out of my mind when this happened." He told Malone what they had seen in the old summerhouse.

"Butch and I took turns watching all night," Helene added. "We didn't see anything, but he's bound to come back there."

"Sure," said Jake, "he forgot his cigarettes."

Malone scowled. "Something needs doing about that."

"Something needs doing about this guy who phoned Dick yesterday and made an appointment with him for three o'clock. But what?" Jake asked.

"Well," said Malone, "I'll get on his trail. You two can't do that because everybody associates you with the Inglehart case. But I can make inquiries without raising suspicion because after all," he said, looking at his watch, "after all, by God, I do have other clients."

"But what about the man in the summerhouse?" Helene asked.

"What about the man or woman who murdered Alexandria

Inglehart?" said Jake. "We can't just leave Holly where she is forever."

"We'll get to that," Malone told him.

"I still think my original idea is good," Helene said. "Jake and I can park in the back room of the garage and watch the summerhouse. If a light shows there, we investigate. If anybody moves, we leap."

"And if anybody leaps, you move," Malone said, "I hope. And if anything turns up out there, get in touch with me."

"We'll send you post cards," Helene promised.

"With pictures of the Blake County jail on them," Malone said, "and an X marking your window." He rose, found his hat under his chair, brushed ineffectively at the ashes on his lapel. "Well, breakfast is on me. I hope it isn't your last." He paid the check and was gone.

They walked out to Helene's car and started north along the drive. The pavement was one wide glistening sheet of ice, almost deserted. For a while they crawled along, watching the great cakes of ice that bobbed up and down in the gray lake.

"You'd think," Jake observed, "they'd make these great big imported cars so they'd go faster than this."

She shook her head. "It makes me terribly nervous to drive when I'm sober."

He remembered that first ride in from Maple Park and shuddered.

"Really," she said thoughtfully, "I'm the safest driver you ever saw. Butch taught me how to control a car in any circumstances. Watch this."

She selected a wide expanse of ice-covered pavement that was entirely deserted, put on a little speed, did sudden and peculiar things with the pedals. The big car suddenly spun around like a top, continued to spin halfway down the block, and, just as suddenly, after four complete revolutions, straightened out and went on as before.

"I wish I could do that with a glass of beer," Helene observed thoughtfully.

Jake felt a strange loneliness where his stomach had been a moment before.

"I rather wish you'd practice with glasses of beer," he told her, "especially when I'm along."

"By God, I've got it! I know now!" The big car slid sideways, missed a lamppost by inches. "Oops, sorry!"

He had hardly noticed. "What is it? What do you know?"

She laughed exuberantly and pounded the wheel in sheer delight.

"Who did it, Helene?"

"Did what?"

"The murder."

"Oh, that. I don't know. Look, Jake, I've got it. The trick is the same with the glass of beer as it is with the car. You reverse it suddenly and—"

He leaned back against the cushions and talked indignantly to God about Helene.

She drove through the Park, turned onto North Clark Street, and stopped the car in front of a little barroom. Jake sighed and followed her in.

"Five beers," said Helene, peeling off her gloves, "and stand aside—"

CHAPTER 21

JAKE STARED unhappily from the rear window of the Brand garage across the expanse of snow and desolation to the Inglehart summerhouse. Butch had cooked them a magnificent dinner in the little kitchen and vanished to tinker with the car. Malone had telephoned the news that he had had no success in tracking down the mysterious man with the yellow gloves, and that there was no word from the missing Dick Dayton.

Jake's spirits had been slowly lowering, were down almost to zero. He glanced now and then at Helene's clear, pallid profile in the semidarkness.

Hell, there was no one in that crazy summerhouse. There wasn't a thing he could do about it if there was. The case was all up in the air. They would never figure it out now. Dick had disappeared, perhaps was dead. Everything was all shot to blazes. For two bits he would walk off that bluff. Yes, by God, he would. But meantime he was here, and Helene was here. That was something.

In fact, it was everything.

He drew her into his arms, touched her cheek with his fingers. Strange that skin looking so delicately cool could be so warm to the touch. A lifetime was short and they had wasted too much of it already.

At that moment his eye caught the faintest gleam of light through the darkness outside the window, a flickering light that moved a little this way and that, a light that vanished and appeared again.

"Jake, somebody's near the summerhouse with a flashlight."

"Yes, I see it."

"What are we going to do?"

"I'm going to investigate. You wait here."

"Wait here my eye!"

"All right then, damn it, come on."

As they stepped into the bitter cold, he could see that the light was in the summerhouse. They crept up to it, slowly and quietly. The light vanished and reappeared through the windows like a firefly as someone moved through the rooms.

Through the window they could see the dim outline of a figure stretched out on the floor.

Then suddenly the light went out, and at the back of the summerhouse a door banged.

"He's seen us!" Jake breathed. He crept around the corner of the low building, Helene behind him.

A man shot from the shelter of the doorway and raced for the lake shore. Jake ran after him, stumbling in the snow, tripping over hidden boulders, while Helene followed as best she could. The air was filled with a thick, heavy mist that seemed to merge into the snow itself.

Jake could hear the roar of the lake as it beat against the jagged rocks of the bluff, and knew that they were near the edge. The man was following the line of the lake shore, almost lost in the mists.

Suddenly he heard a cry behind him and wheeled just in time to see Helene topple and fall. Before he could reach her she had slipped halfway over the edge of the cliff. He threw himself full length on the snow, grasped her wrists just as she fell, and held her there for a moment. A sharp rock under the snow was the miracle that kept him from going over with her.

"Try to get a foothold," he gasped.

Inch by inch he hauled her over the edge. For one terrible moment he felt her slipping from him and clung to her desperately, the sharp rocks bruising his arms and wrists. Then she gained a firmer foothold, little by little was dragged back to safety.

For a moment he stood looking at her as she lay exhausted in the snow, thinking that her face was only a shade less pale than the snow itself, and that if she had gone over the cliff, he would have gone with her.

"I'm all right, Jake. I can get up now." She managed to get to her feet. "But that man. He's gone. We lost him."

"It doesn't matter, Helene. As long as you're all right, it doesn't matter."

She leaned against him for an instant and he put his arm around her very gently.

"First a laundry chute," he murmured in a disgusted tone, "and then you fell off a cliff."

Her eyes looked over his shoulder, suddenly grew wide. He turned around.

Ahead of them stood the man from the summerhouse, hazy and unreal in the shifting vapor, but clear enough so that they could see what was in his hand.

"Stay right where you are. Don't come any nearer."

"Don't point that damn gun this way," Jake shouted.

"Stay where you are," the man repeated.

Jake said, "Who the hell are you, and what are you doing here?"

An eerie laugh came through the quiet night. "You want to know a lot."

"We sure do."

"I'll tell you this much. You're the people *I* want to see."

"Jake, for God's sake," Helene whispered.

The figure moved a little closer through the mist.

"What do you want?" Jake called.

"It's not what I want, it's what you want. You want to know who killed Alexandria Inglehart."

"The man's mad!" Helene murmured.

"Shut up, damn you," he whispered fiercely. "Do you know?"

No answer save that weird laugh through the mist.

"How do you know?" Jake shouted.

"I was there. I'm the man who opened the window. Didn't you wonder why the window was opened? I opened it."

Jake felt Helene's hand in his, like a sliver of ice.

"And I know why she was murdered, why she had to be killed, and that's the most important thing. I know the motive."

"All right, what was it?" Jake called.

"The motive? *I* was the motive," laughed the dim figure.

A whisper. "Jake, what are we going to do?"

And then. "How much is my information worth to you?" came the voice through the mist.

"So that's it," Jake muttered. "How much do you want?" he called.

"A thousand dollars in cash. No checks."

"Tell him yes," Helene whispered.

"I heard you, Miss Brand," came the floating voice. "I'll take your offer."

"Just a minute," Helene called. "How will we know you're telling the truth?"

"I'll bring proof."

"Where?"

"The summerhouse. Ten tomorrow morning."

"It's a deal," Helene called.

"Wait a minute," Jake shouted. "First turn that flashlight on yourself and let us have a look at you—so that we'll know you tomorrow."

After a moment's hesitation there was a flash of light in the mist and the figure stood revealed. They saw an oddly dapper little man, not the tramplike creature they had expected. Derby hat, Chesterfield overcoat, waxed mustache—all oddly incongruous in the setting of snow and ice-packed boulders. Then in an instant it was gone, the light went out, and the eerie figure had vanished.

"Was it real," Helene gasped, "or something we dreamed!"

"It was real enough," said Jake grimly, "and something else is real, too. There was someone on the floor of the summerhouse. We may have discovered another murder."

"Jake! That man! Did you recognize him?"

"Never saw him before in my life."

"You fool! He's the man that bartender described to us—the one who telephoned to Dick!"

"By God, you're right!"

"Then—Dick—"

"That body in the summerhouse," said Jake harshly. "Come on, let's go."

They fought their way through the snowdrifts to the summerhouse. The door was locked. Jake battered vainly against it for a few minutes, gave it up, bashed a rock through the nearest window, reached through the shattered pane, opened the window, and climbed in. Helene followed him.

"Helene, perhaps you'd better stay outside."

"I'm in already. Don't be a dope."

"Dark as the bottom of a well in here."

He fumbled for a match, found one, struck it, discovered a lantern on the table and lighted it. The flame flickered and grew brighter; in its glow they could see the body that lay on its face on the floor. It was the body of a tall, blond young man. A dark patch of dried blood stained the side of his head.

Jake rolled the body over and looked into the still, colorless face of Dick Dayton.

CHAPTER 22

Butch, hastily summoned, helped carry the injured man to the garage, laid him on the bed in his own room.

"Helene, do you know a doctor who can keep his mouth shut—and get here in a hurry?"

She nodded. "Doc Kendall. Phone him, Butch. Jake, do you think we ought to call the police?"

"Not at this stage of the game."

"But if Dick should die—"

"He won't die," said Jake savagely.

"But how did he get out here?"

"On skis, probably," Jake said, lighting a cigarette.

"Jake, please."

"Hell, I don't know what happened. Dick can tell us when he comes to. My guess is that this mysterious little dude lured Dick out here with the same offer he made to us."

"But then why should he knock him out?"

"Maybe he didn't like his face."

"I'm beginning not to like yours, Jake Justus."

"Well, probably Dick tried to pull a fast one. Must have. He didn't draw any dough out of the bank before he disappeared, because we checked the bank first thing. He tried to pull a fast one, and the little guy bopped him."

"Dick must have lain there for hours," Helene said thoughtfully "If we hadn't arrived just when we did—"

"Didn't you know? I'm a marine."

"Isn't there anything we could be doing for him?"

"Not until your doctor gets here, and I hope he's a good one."

"He is. He pulled Butch through once when somebody shot him."

"Intentionally?" Jake asked politely.

"Jake, do you think that man murdered Aunt Alex?"

"Possibly."

"What do you think he meant when he said he was the motive?"

"I don't know."

"Do you think he really has anything to tell us?"

"I don't know."

She became tactfully silent.

At last the doctor arrived, a plump, bustling man with a friendly, anxious face.

"What have you gotten yourself into this time, Helene?"

She waved silently toward the still figure on the bed. The doctor looked and whistled.

"How did you do it?"

"I didn't do it. We found him."

The doctor gave a closer look.

"Good God, Helene. Do you know who this is?"

She nodded. "You're damned right I do. That's why I sent for you—you know how to keep your mouth shut. Jake, you tell him the works."

Jake told the story as briefly as possible while the doctor

worked over Dick. They finished at about the same time. Dr. Kendall nodded understandingly.

"You see," said Helene, "you see why it has to be kept quiet."

"And Dick," said Jake, "is he—I mean—how is he?"

"He'll be all right. Nasty crack on the bean. A few more hours without attention might have been bad."

"How long before he'll be able to tell us what happened?"

"Can't say."

Jake groaned.

"Maybe tomorrow, maybe next day, maybe longer. You'll have to have patience. You also ought to have a nurse."

"How about Butch?" Helene asked.

"He'll do all right. He's a good nurse."

The doctor gave instructions to Butch, promised to look in the next morning, told them not to worry, and went away.

Jake turned to Helene. All of them, even the doctor, had been much too concerned with Dick Dayton to notice her. Her face was a chalky white, her pale blond hair was tangled about her shoulders. Her dress, stained with mud and snow, hung in shreds. There was, he saw for the first time, an ugly scratch on her forehead.

"You look like you'd had a fall, or something," he said laconically.

He caught her just as she swayed and fell, and laid her gently on the couch of the little living room. Butch came with hot water, they bathed the cuts and bruises, poured brandy between her bluish lips. After what seemed a very long time she opened her eyes momentarily, murmured an incoherent something, smiled at Jake, tucked her hand under her cheek, and quietly went to sleep.

Jake put blankets over her, laid a hot-water bottle against her feet.

"Don't worry," he told Butch, "the chances are she won't get anything worse than double pneumonia."

He stood looking at her for a long time. Her face in sleep was the smooth, contented face of a tired child; her fragile, slim-fingered hand nestled under her chin, her long eyelashes curved against the cool pallor of her cheeks.

At last he kissed her, very gently, on the forehead, and turned quietly away.

But the night was not over.

He looked out the window. The mist was lifting, and suddenly, darkly silhouetted against the snow, he could see the figure of a man making his way from the Inglehart house to the summerhouse on the cliff. It was not the dapper little man.

Then who was it?

The figure looked faintly familiar. Glen? No. But still familiar.

He decided it was best to investigate, raced down the stairs, through the stone gate, and across the snow-covered lawn. The man saw him, stopped, turned, and ran back toward the Inglehart house, but not quickly enough. In a few strides Jake had caught up with him, grabbed him by the shoulders, swung him around.

Parkins!

The mild little man was white with terror.

"Oh Mr. Justus—let me go—"

"I will not," said Jake Justus, shaking the frightened man like a rat. "I will not. I know where you were going. Who's been staying in that summerhouse?"

Parkins gulped. "Nobody, sir."

"Tell me, or I'll break every bone in your body."

"The summerhouse, sir—the summerhouse, it hasn't been used for years. There can't be anyone staying there."

"Yes there is, Parkins. I saw him there tonight."

Parkins' face was a mask, in spite of his fright. "I know nothing about it, sir, nothing whatever."

"Listen, you blithering fool, don't you want to help Miss Holly? Don't you want to help get her out of trouble?"

"Oh, yes, sir. You know I do, sir."

"Well, so do I. I'm trying to help her. That's why I've got to know who is staying in the summerhouse."

There was no answer.

"Tell me who it is, or so help me, I'll go straight to the police. And they'll find out who it is. I'll do it, Parkins, I warn you."

Parkins looked at him squarely. "That might be the best thing to do, Mr. Justus."

Jake loosened his hold on the little man, who turned in a flash and scuttled back to the house like a terrified rabbit.

Well, evidently he'd get no information from Parkins that way. But the little man knew something. Malone would know a way to pry it out of him.

He walked slowly back to the garage.

It was even possible that Parkins was telling the truth. Not probable, though. Just how did he figure in the tangle? What kind of game was he playing?

How much did Mrs. Parkins know about it?

Who was the little dude in the summerhouse?

Back in the garage, Jake resumed his vigil at the window.

Whoever the little dude was, the chances were that he would return to the summerhouse. He would discover that it had been entered and that Dick had been taken away.

And then would he be frightened and bolt?

No, he would know who had taken Dick away, and that they would hardly go to the police with their information. In any case, there was nothing to do but wait for the next morning's appointment.

It was about nine o'clock that he saw a faint flicker of light along the lake shore, a moment later, a light showed in the summerhouse. The stranger had returned. Jake watched a few minutes longer. Evidently the man had decided to stay.

He tried to phone John J. Malone, but the lawyer could not be located. Jake left a trail of messages for him, each telling him to come to the garage early in the morning. Then he tiptoed into the room where Butch sat watching the unconscious young man in the bed. There was no change in his condition.

Helene still slept, smiling faintly in her sleep.

Should he keep up his watch by the window? No, he decided, there was nothing to watch for now. Everyone had settled down for the night. The hell with the window. The hell with the guy in the summerhouse. The hell with everything. He was going to get some sleep.

He selected a couch, rolled himself up in a blanket, and was dead to the world in thirty seconds.

He had no way of knowing, but if he had watched by the window a few minutes later, he might have seen much, learned a great deal, even prevented a few things.

Certainly the Inglehart case would have been closed much sooner if he had kept on watching by the window.

But Jake slept.

CHAPTER 23

"Did you fall, or were you pushed?" asked Jake sympathetically.

Helene moaned faintly and turned her face to the wall. "My mother always told me there'd be days like this, but she didn't tell me I'd live to see them." She stretched and winced. "Who or what threw me, and where, and at what?"

"I did," Jake said, "over a cliff."

"Oh, I remember now." She sat up and wrapped the blanket around her pale shoulders. "I seem to go to sleep in the damnedest places."

"And at the damnedest times," Jake reminded her.

"How's the patient?"

"Dick? He's just the same. Malone's on his way out."

"That man is always running in on me when I've just gotten out of bed." She began fussing with her hair. "How do I look, anyway?"

"Terrible," he lied.

She looked at her watch. "We meet the little dude at ten o'clock. Why does everything happen so early in the morning? And I've got to go to the bank first."

"Why should you do the kicking-in?"

"This is no time to argue about who pays the street-car fare. I'll get it back some day."

He regarded her thoughtfully. "If I weren't a broken-down press agent and you weren't a beautiful blonde heiress, and I thought we'd be happy together, I'd probably propose to you, but I am and you are and we wouldn't be, so I won't."

"Thanks."

"But just the same, once we get this damn murder cleared up and people aren't interrupting us all the time, and it looks as though we might have an evening to ourselves—"

Just then John J. Malone arrived.

Jake told him of the night's adventures while Helene proudly exhibited her bruises.

Butch brought in a tray of breakfast.

"Why kick in with the cash?" Malone asked. "Let's simply go down there and lay for him—"

Jake shook his head. "Won't work. He's a wary little bird. No, we'll go down there cash in hand and get his story. Then we'll nab him."

"What do you think he has to tell?" Helene asked.

"If I knew that, I'd be selling it to you myself," Jake said bitterly.

"You know," she said, "I've been thinking. Glen and Maybelle. Pa Parkins. Pa might feel that as Maybelle's father he ought to do something matrimonial about the family honor. But he might also have felt that Aunt Alex would never let anything matrimonial take place. Do you follow me?"

"With some difficulty."

"So Parkins and Maybelle dish this up. Maybelle does the imitating of Holly's voice. Having known Holly all her life, she could do it and get away with it. Then she or Parkins does the actual murder."

"You forget," Jake said, "Parkins wouldn't have a chance to get back to the house and do the murder, because Glen was with him all the time."

"Maybe Glen was in it too."

"Then why go through all this monkeyshining to lure him away? And do you think he really wanted to marry Maybelle?"

"He might not have anything to say about it if Parkins really had his dander up."

"I don't see Parkins in a coonskin cap with a gun under his arm."

"All right, Glen wasn't in the plot. Parkins was mad at Aunt Alex for picking on Maybelle, and he did it all by himself."

"But how did Parkins get back to the house and do the murder?"

"This is the point where it gets a little too involved for me," she said.

"And," said Jake, "it doesn't explain where Holly was all the time. Or why this guy in the summerhouse says he's the motive."

"That," said Helene crisply, "is the part I was leaving for you to figure out."

"Have a few more ideas," Malone said, "and maybe we'll hit on a good one."

"Holly!" said a cracked and terrible voice behind him. "What have you done with her?"

Dick Dayton was standing in the doorway, hanging on to the door for support, his face a ghastly gray under its bandage.

"For Christ's sake," Jake said, "get back in that bed."

"Holly!"

"She's safe. We've got her hidden." He tried to lead Dick back to the bedroom. "Lie down. You've got a concussion."

"I hope it's contagious," Dick said angrily, "and I hope you get it." He pushed Jake aside, staggered in to the couch, and sat down heavily. "What's happened? I seem to have been away for a while."

"What happened to you?"

"I guess I did a fool thing," Dick said. "There was this phone call. I tried to get in touch with you, Jake, but I couldn't. I knew I had to do something about it. The phone call, I mean. You couldn't just not do anything about something like that. Anyway the end of the Michigan Avenue Bridge ought to be the safest place in the world. So why shouldn't I have gone there? I guess," he said, scowling, "I guess I'm not much good at telling things."

"Maybe you could play it on a clarinet," Jake said disgustedly.

Malone decided to help. "Pick up the story at the bridge, Dayton. Did this man meet you there?"

Dick nodded.

"What did he look like?"

Dick gave them a fair description of the man of the summerhouse. "He told me that he'd been in—in that room the night of the murder. He told me that he knew who had done it and why. But that he didn't want to be seen talking to me."

"And he wanted you to go out to the summerhouse with him?" Malone prompted.

"No, he wanted me to meet him there later. He said he had all the proof. He wanted me to get a thousand dollars and meet him there."

"He sticks to the same price," Helene murmured.

"But you didn't take the money?" Jake asked.

"No. It—well, I guess it was a mistake. I thought maybe I could—well, he was a little guy. I was going to turn him over to you."

"But he got you first?"

A puzzled look came into Dick's eyes. "No. He didn't. That's the funny thing."

"What *did* happen?" Jake asked desperately.

"Well, the summerhouse wasn't locked. I went in and sat down and waited for him. Then I saw this guy coming down the path. He came in the door on the lake side of the house, and then came into the room where I was waiting. I saw him come through the door." He paused. "This is the part I don't understand."

"For the love of God," Jake began.

"He stopped in the doorway a minute. And he looked startled. I remember that terribly well, how startled he looked. Because that's the last thing I remember. Because just then something struck my head and that's all I remember."

For a while it seemed as though something had struck all of them and left them speechless.

"You mean," said Malone after he had found his voice, "you mean this man in the summerhouse wasn't the one who knocked you cold?"

"How could he be when I was looking at him at the time?"

"The answer seems to be that he wasn't," Jake said after a pause.

"But then," said Helene, "who did?"

No one had any suggestions.

"I want to go see Holly," Dick said.

Jake shook his head. "You're staying in bed for a while."

"I'm perfectly all right. And I haven't seen Holly since—not for days and days."

This time Malone shook his head. "In broad daylight, with every cop in Chicago looking for you? Do you want to get Holly put back in jail? I didn't think you did. Then don't go leading them right to her door."

"Patience is a wonderful thing," Helene added. She looked at her watch. "Jesus!" she remarked. "Back in half an hour."

"What do you think of her idea about the Parkinses?" Jake asked Malone after she had gone.

The little lawyer shook his head. "I don't know. It's impossible the way she figured it. But they're mixed up in it somehow." He paused to struggle with a shoelace. "I wish I knew what she's keeping back."

"You mean Helene?"

"I don't mean Greta Garbo," Malone said. "Helene is keeping secrets from me. So is Glen Inglehart. I suspect they're the same secrets."

"Well," Jake said thoughtfully, "I could ask her."

Malone looked at him with disgust. "Hell, that girl could make you believe Hoover was still president."

"Give me that girl," said Jake piously, "and I'd run for president myself." He frowned. "Malone, you don't think she murdered the old dame?"

"I don't know. I only know that in a case like this I'm interested in the people who are lying to me. Because there's usually a reason for it. She's lying to me, and Glen is, and both the Parkinses. Why?"

"Malone, why did the little dude in the summerhouse say he was the motive?"

"Why indeed?" said Malone mildly.

" 'I'm the motive,' he said, and then he laughed. What did he mean, Malone? He knew something about Holly. That was it."

Malone took it up from there. "He knew something about Holly. Something that would queer her with her Aunt Alex. She was afraid to tackle him, but she thought she could get away with wiping out the old lady. No, it doesn't work that way either. Because she knew she was going to be queered, and permanently, as soon as the news of her marriage was made public."

"Maybe he knew something about Glen," Jake suggested. "Glen and Maybelle Parkins."

"No," Malone said, "because the old dame knew about that anyway."

"He said he was the guy who opened the window. Where was Holly while he was opening the window? Why did he open the window?"

"Maybe he wanted fresh air."

"Maybe he wanted to lean out and catch birds," said Jake in disgust. "Hell, I'm going to get myself shaved and cleaned up, if I can borrow Butch's razor. This kind of life is wearing me down."

Helene returned a little before ten, regal and spectacular in a deep green suit, with immense bands of thick brown fur, and a wide green hat that formed a frame around her pale face.

"Have you the dough?"

She showed them an envelope with ten crisp hundred-dollar bills. "The cashier at the bank believes I'm being blackmailed."

They decided that Malone should accompany them to the fringe of trees that hedged in the old summerhouse and wait there, out of sight. If anything went wrong, they would signal to him from the window.

Jake and Helene walked on in silence. Snow had been falling in little flurries since early morning; now it was coming down in earnest, settling heavily on the leafless branches and dark bushes. She took his arm and held it, very tight.

"Scared?"

She shook her head. "Excited. Jake, what do you think he'll tell us?"

"Everything, I hope."

"Half an hour from now we'll know what happened, and why."

"And then," Jake said, "and then—"

She pressed his hand.

They rapped lightly on the summerhouse door and waited. There was no answer. They rapped again, louder.

"Think he's run out on us?" Helene whispered.

"I don't know." He tried the door, it was unlocked. He pushed it open, slowly.

"No one here."

"Maybe we're early," Jake said.

Helene stood looking around her. "Everything looks just the way it did last night."

"How the hell else did you expect it to look?"

"I mean, it looks as if he's still living here."

"Wait," Jake said, "I'm going to look around a little."

He pushed open the door that led into a little kitchen, looked around, came back shaking his head, and went into the long room that fronted on the lake. He was gone for only an instant, and when he returned he walked to the open door of the summerhouse and bawled loudly for Malone.

The little lawyer came puffing through the snow.

"What have you found, Jake?"

"Come in here—yes, both of you."

They followed him into a bare, unfurnished room.

There on the floor, among the dust and the cobwebs, lay the body of the little dude.

Malone knelt beside the body, examined it hastily. "Dead for hours."

"How?" Jake asked.

"Stabbed. And—yes, by God—there are three wounds. Three."

They were silent for a moment.

"Look," said Helene in a curiously flat voice. "Look, Malone. Has he a watch?"

"Yes," Malone told her after a pause. "A wrist watch." He rolled up the dead man's cuff.

They bent over his shoulder to look, knowing, and yet not daring to believe, what they would see.

The dead man's watch had stopped.

Its hands pointed to three o'clock.

CHAPTER 24

HELENE'S FACE was very pale, but her voice was steady. "Who did it, Malone? Same guy that did in Aunt Alex?"

"Same guy," said Malone, "or somebody trying to make it look like the same guy." He looked up at them. "This affair seems to go by threes. Three wounds in each corpse. The clocks stopped at three. Maybe we'd better move fast."

"Why?"

"Before there's three murders."

"Move fast," Jake said, "when we're right back where we started. This poor little guy isn't going to tell us a thing."

"Maybe he is," Malone said.

He began a slow and systematic inspection. Wrapping a handkerchief around his fingers he examined the knife. It was an ordinary kitchen knife.

"Buy one at any hardware store," Malone said.

He searched the dead man's pockets. There was a package of papers; he flipped through them and struck them in his own pocket.

"We'll look these over later."

Then he came to the wallet. It was a new wallet, brand new. In it was a fat sheaf of bills.

Malone counted them. "Three hundred and fifty six dollars," he reported.

"You know," Jake said, "I notice something. All that guy's clothes are new. Not just his suit and his overcoat and his shoes, but everything. Hat, shirt, ties, socks—probably his underwear too. Now that's funny. A guy usually doesn't buy all new clothes at one time."

"Disguising himself," Helene suggested.

"Much simpler than that," said Malone; "he'd just come into money."

"Selling his information to somebody else?" Jake asked.

"Much more likely that he's been blackmailing somebody."

"Who?"

"Probably whoever murdered Alexandria Inglehart," Malone said. He finished searching the body, looked at it speculatively for a moment, then began systematically removing every mark of identification.

"What are you doing that for?"

"No real reason. Just giving the local cops something to do in their spare time."

Finally he searched the little summerhouse, found nothing of importance, and indicated that he was ready to go.

"Did either of you touch anything in here?"

They shook their heads.

"Just as well. Someone may have told Blake County about fingerprints."

They went out into the snow.

"But look here," Helene said, "look here. What are we going to do about that guy? We can't just leave him there."

"We aren't going to."

"Are you going to tell the police?"

"No. But Parkins is."

"Parkins?" she repeated stupidly.

Malone nodded silently. Helene turned helplessly to Jake.

"There's no use talking to him when he's like this," Jake said.

She sighed. "I think we'd better go back to the garage and have a drink," she said.

"I think you're right," Malone said.

Dick turned very white at the news they had for him. "Then you aren't going to learn anything from him."

"No," Jake said, "but we've learned one thing that ought to make you feel better. This proves conclusively that Holly didn't murder her aunt."

"It doesn't prove a damned thing," Malone said indignantly.

"She couldn't possibly have committed this murder," Jake said. "And this man was killed by the same person who murdered the old woman."

"Or, as I said, someone who wanted to make it look like the same person," Malone said.

"Still, it makes sense. This little dude knew who had done the original crime. He was blackmailing the murderer. He was rubbed out in just the same way. That's proof enough for me."

"As far as I'm concerned," Dick said, "I don't need any proof that Holly is innocent."

"But you aren't Blake County," Malone said.

Jake muttered an impolite inquiry regarding Malone's parentage.

Malone ignored him. "There's someone," he said after a pause, "someone who lured Glen and the Parkinses out of the house by a phony call from Holly, got Holly out of the house in a way that she doesn't remember, stabbed Alexandria Inglehart, knocked Dick on the head just as the little dude was going to tell him a few things, and finally stabbed the little dude last night. And that someone is still running around loose, and we still don't know who it is."

"And things go by three," Helene said, "and we've had two murders already."

Malone nodded. "It's this way," he said slowly. "Either it's you, Helene, or Glen, or Holly, or one of the three Parkinses. Or else it's someone we know nothing about."

"I wish I knew what it was I thought of, but I've forgotten it," said Jake sorrowfully.

"What are you mumbling about?"

"I thought of something. Night before last. Something important. And I haven't been able to think of it since."

"He had an idea," said Helene, "but it went from him."

They looked at him anxiously.

"Were you drunk or sober when you thought of it?" Malone asked.

"Drunk," said Jake.

There was a half bottle of rye on the table. He eyed it speculatively for a moment, uncapped it, picked up a glass, discarded it, and lifted the bottle to his lips.

Helene counted softly under her breath.

"Thirty seconds by the clock!"

He stared at her.

"By God," said Jake, "by God, I do remember!" He wiped his chin.

A light broke over her face. "Wait. So do I. You muttered something about clocks."

"That's it!" He turned to Malone, his eyes flickering with excitement. "What stopped all those damned clocks?"

The lawyer looked at him stupidly.

"The clocks," Jake repeated. "You know. Tick-tock, tick-tock. All of the clocks—stopped at three. You know what I'm talking about, damn you. The clocks."

"Of course I know what you're talking about."

"What made them stop? What made them stop all at once like that?"

The silence could almost be felt, like a cold wind in the room.

"I don't know," said Malone after a while.

"Clocks don't just stop of their own accord," Jake said.

"But these did."

"Why? Malone, that's something we've got to find out. It's the most important thing. It's the key to something. Perhaps the key to everything. We've got to find out what made all those clocks stop, every clock in the house, simultaneously, at three."

"If we ever can find out," said Malone slowly. "I mean, if it's within the human power of finding out."

"I don't like the tone of your voice," Helene said with a little shudder.

"There's some things that can't be explained," Malone said.

"But surely," Jake began, and stopped. "But surely!" again. "You don't believe—I mean you, an educated man, certainly can't think—well damn it all, Malone, you can't ask us to believe any infernal nonsense like that."

"It may be nonsense," Malone told him, "but it sure as hell would be infernal."

"Oh, no," Helene said. Her face was pale. "Malone, it can't be. Things like that simply aren't."

"All right. You explain it."

"Thanks," she answered, "I'd rather not. Clocks don't stop all over a house when an old woman is murdered. Even if it's true, I don't believe it."

"The grandfather's clock—" Dick began, and stopped.

"What about the grandfather's clock?" Jake asked.

"I was thinking of the song."

"The man's delirious," Helene murmured.

"I am not delirious," Dick said irritably. "I said I was thinking of the song, and I am. Grandfather's clock." He hummed a moment, suddenly sang, "But it stopped—short—never to go again—when the old man died."

"That's what I meant," Malone said. "That's it. There is a superstition about clocks stopping when someone dies."

"And you believe it?" Jake asked incredulously.

"I didn't say I believed it," Malone said crossly. "I believe that there is such a superstition and that someone tried to take advantage of it."

"What do you mean?" Helene asked. "Do you know what stopped the clocks?"

"Not yet," Malone said, "not yet, I don't. But," he added grimly, "I'm sure as hell going to find out!"

CHAPTER 25

PARKINS, LOOKING haggard and pale, informed them that Glen had gone into town.

"That's all right," Malone said, "we just want to go over the house."

"Of course, sir. If I can be of any help—"

"We'll call you."

They climbed the stairs to Holly's room. It had been left just as it had been found the night of the murder. The narrow bed with its soft, peach-colored cover was smooth and neat. They searched the room, found nothing of interest, examined the closet, a dark, narrow slot of a room with an overhead bar for coat hangers. Nothing there. Nothing of meaning in the whole room save that smooth, unrumpled bed and the little onyx clock on the table.

Malone looked speculatively at the clock, slipped it into his pocket.

"Where did she go from here?"

"Glen's room," said Helene, "down the hall."

They went down the hall to a neat, bare room where a silver-framed photograph of Helene occupied the central position on the dresser. Helene reflectively drew a small trim beard and mustache on the picture glass with her eyebrow pencil.

There was nothing of interest in Glen's room either. Save the clock, the sturdy little leather clock. It had not been touched since that night, its luminous hands still pointed to three. Malone tucked it in his pocket and they filed silently out.

There was the clock in the hall, the old mahogany wall clock, standing just as it had stood when Holly looked at it. Malone examined it carefully.

"I hope he doesn't try to slip that in his pocket," Jake muttered. "Is the man a clocktomaniac?"

They trailed along the hall, up the narrow back stairs to the Parkins' room. There was one more clock, the cheap alarm clock, the alarm clock that hadn't rung. Malone hung its ring over the end of his finger and sauntered out.

There was a little enameled clock on a table in the hall.

"My God," Jake exploded, "the place is alive with clocks."

"Alive with dead clocks," Helene said.

They paused for a moment at the door of the room that had been Miss Alexandria Inglehart's.

The room was very still. Nothing stirred there, nothing was alive. Not even the gold clock in the bell glass, standing there on the greenish marble mantel, with its tiny wheel that stood so motionless, its fragile, filigree hands pointing to three.

The little French clock had ticked away the hours of Alexandria Inglehart's life, hour and day and week and year. Then someone had plunged a knife three times into Alexandria Inglehart's withered old bosom, and the clock had stopped, suddenly, dead still. At three o'clock.

And all the other clocks in the house.

"Let's go downstairs," Malone said in a strangely flat voice.

He led the way to the library, where they laid the clocks in a neat row on the table.

"I want one more. The electric clock." Malone looked around. It stood on a table against the wall, its hands still pointing to three. He walked over and examined it.

"Jake, come look at this."

"What?"

"See?" He pointed to the wall plug. "It's still hitched up. But it isn't going. And the other electric fixtures seem to be going all right."

"Judas!" said Jake, "that *is* crazy as hell. Because I know that make of clock. When they're plugged in, practically nothing can stop them. But that clock is plugged in all right, and it's stopped dead."

Malone muttered something unintelligible, yanked the plug from its socket and added the polished-wood electric clock to his collection.

Then he settled down to a slow and painstaking examination.

First he looked at Holly's little onyx clock, shook it, and made experimental motions among the keys at its back. Then with a satisfied grunt he laid it down and went on to the next clock.

Jake and Helene watched with silent impatience.

At last he had finished with all but the electric clock. He examined it with unusual care, ran his fingers back and forth on the length of electric wire, finally began loosening the screws of the wall plug.

"Jake," he began slowly, "what happens when you wind a clock too tight?"

"It stops," Jake said promptly, "and you have to take it to the repair shop to get it started again."

"Exactly," the lawyer murmured, still fiddling with the wall plug.

Jake picked up one of the clocks and tried to twist the winding key. It was stuck fast. He tried another, it was the same.

"What the hell?"

"Look at this," Malone said. He held out the plug.

"It's disconnected—inside the plug—where it wouldn't show."

Malone nodded. "I don't know yet how the other clocks were stopped—that gilt contraption upstairs, or the hall clock—but I've no doubt that I'd make the same discovery—some little thing that would effectively stop a clock—as simple and as effective as winding these clocks too tight, or breaking the connection in a wall plug."

He tossed the plug carelessly on the table. "No, it wasn't any supernatural power that stopped all the clocks or the wrist watch on that poor little guy."

"Someone stopped them," Helene said. "On purpose. Deliberately. But who?"

"Probably the person who murdered Alexandria Inglehart."

"But why?" said Jake blankly. "What was the idea? Why go around advertising the time of the murder like that? Unless there was some reason for wanting the world to know that the old woman died at exactly three."

"There is a reason," Malone told him, "only we don't know what it is. It all fits into some kind of pattern, only we can't see what the pattern is yet. What's the matter, Helene?"

"Wait. I'm thinking of something." She was examining the

enameled clock. "Listen. There can't be any doubt. These clocks were all stopped by some human hand—someone who went all through the house deliberately stopping every clock, from the French clock in Aunt Alex's room to the electric clock here, not even missing the alarm clock in the Parkins' room. That's true, isn't it, Malone? There can't be any doubt?"

"Not a doubt in the world," Malone said.

"You two big lugs. You're missing the most important thing these clocks have to tell you. They're trying their damnedest to tell you what it is and here you sit like a pair of dopes."

"What in hell are you talking about?" Jake growled.

"Listen. Suppose you started, exactly at three o'clock, at the top of this house and went straight through it, stopping to put every clock you found out of commission—*what time would it be when you got to the last clock?*"

"My God," said Jake after a long silence.

"The first clock," said Malone, slowly and meditatively, "would have been three, exactly. The next, a couple of minutes past three, and the next perhaps five minutes past three, and so on, unless—"

"Unless," Helene finished for him, "you turned the hands of each clock back to three when you stopped it, which is obviously what this mysterious bird did do. And that bit of information points to something else, which you two guys may be able to see for yourselves."

"You're damned right we see it," said Malone bitterly. "And it knocks everything sky-high. So far everybody has been going on the theory that Alexandria Inglehart died at three o'clock, and every clock in the house promptly stopped. Now we know a hell of a lot less than we did when we got here."

"The clocks could have been stopped at any time," Jake said, "at three o'clock or at two o'clock or—well, any damn time. At the time of the murder or before it or after it."

Helene sighed. "We all simply leaped to the conclusion that Aunt Alex met her Maker on the dot of three. It's even possible that she did."

"There's just one thing we do know about the time of her death," Malone said grimly. "It comes somewhere in the time between the hour when Glen and Parkins left the house—when the old woman was still alive—and the hour when Glen and the Parkinses came back."

"Between the hour when Glen and Parkins left the house," Jake said, "and the time when Holly walked into her aunt's room and found the body."

"All right," Malone said, "we'll go on that theory. But we don't know what time it was when Holly went into the room."

"Except that it was sometime after three," Jake began, and stopped. "No, we don't know that either."

"No. Because the clock-stopping might have been done at any time, as far as we know." Malone groaned heavily. He searched through his pockets, finally located a half-eaten pencil and an old envelope.

"Let's try to get some sense out of this. Glen and Parkins left the house a little after eleven. Call it eleven-fifteen. They came back a little before four. Let's call it quarter to four. All right. That leaves us four hours and a half. The old lady was dead when they got back. So obviously the murder—and all this damned monkey-doodling with the clocks—took place between eleven-fifteen and a quarter to four. There, by God, we know something definite."

"Who has what alibis for that four and a half hours?" Helene asked.

"Well, let's see. Start with Holly," Jake said.

"Holly—question mark," Malone said. "Dick Dayton?"

"In view of two or three hundred people at the Casino," Jake said. "I was there until about three-thirty. And I couldn't have gotten here before four if I'd used a rocket ship. You'll have to check us both off the list."

"Too bad," Malone muttered. "I've been hoping for years to pin something on you. All right—Glen and the Parkinses. They were driving to Chicago and back. There's no doubt about that. Even if the three of them were in cahoots and were all lying, their story was checked with an attendant at St. Luke's Hospital."

"And that leaves—?" Jake asked.

"Helene. Helene, where were you at three o'clock?"

Helene started. "As a matter of honest-to-God fact, I have no alibi in the world. I was out driving."

"You could have done it," Malone said. "You could have called up and imitated Holly's voice and gotten away with it, too, after knowing her all your life. And you could have gotten into the house—you admitted you have a key."

"Motive?" Jake asked.

"When you've known me long enough," she said, "you'll probably find I have a motive for damn near anything."

There was a silence.

"Only"—she frowned—"only it doesn't explain where Holly was all that time."

"It doesn't explain a lot of things," Jake said.

Malone scowled. "Well, we learned something anyway. And we'll keep it to ourselves for a while. Let Blake County go on believing that she was killed at three o'clock."

"Damn it," Jake said, "we get back to the theory that this was done by an outsider. Maybe the little dude, and then someone murdered him. Or someone we haven't caught up with yet."

"Either that, or Holly," said Malone wearily.

There were heavy steps in the hall.

With remarkable presence of mind, Helene hopped up on the library table and spread the heavily furred skirts of her coat over the clocks. Malone adroitly kicked the electric clock under the table.

In the next moment the library door opened and in walked Hyme Mendel and the pessimistic Mr. Fleck.

CHAPTER 26

LATER HELENE declared that never before in her life had she understood just how a setting hen felt. Any minute, she said, she expected one of the infernal clocks to hatch, probably a cuckoo. It was a difficult few minutes.

It would have been difficult even without the clocks.

Hyme Mendel wore the look of a man who has been exasperated just a little beyond human endurance. In addition, Jake suspected, he had a hang-over.

Had he discovered the murder of the man in the summerhouse, Jake wondered. Or had he discovered that the man was staying there, and would he go down that snow-covered slope in another minute to find the man dead?

And if he did—what?

Hyme Mendel was glaring at Malone. "Well," he said explosively, "I'm certainly glad to see *you!*"

He didn't look it.

John J. Malone raised his right eyebrow. "Something?"

"Damned well something, and you damned well know it." The angry young man seemed to be uncomfortably full of words. "Where have you got her?"

"Got who?" Malone said mildly.

"He means Miss Inglehart," Jasper Fleck said helpfully.

"Mrs. Dayton," Hyme Mendel corrected him.

"But I haven't got her," Malone said in a hurt voice.

"How did you get her away from here?" Mendel asked.

"I didn't get her away from here," Malone told him, "and I haven't got her. I don't know where she is. In fact," he added, "I wish to God I did."

"Nuts!" said Hyme Mendel indignantly. It seemed to relieve his feelings.

"If you care to," Malone went on, "you can check on all my movements the evening of the jailbreak. Or rather, her escape. Not technically a jailbreak since she didn't actually get out of jail. In any case, you'll find that I couldn't possibly have had anything to do with it. And I didn't. So help me God, I didn't know a thing about it until I read it in the papers the next day."

Hyme Mendel stared at him. "Are you telling me the truth?"

"Of course I'm telling you the truth."

Hyme Mendel looked suspiciously at Helene, who was wondering why the Parkinses had to have such a big alarm clock.

"Miss Brand—"

"Surely," she said, looking at him with very wide eyes, "you can't think I had anything to do with it. You remember Mr. Justus and I were right here all the time, and we even helped you hunt for her."

"But if you knew where she was—"

"If I knew where she was," Helene said, "wouldn't you think I'd tell Mr. Malone, when I'm doing my best to help him?"

Hyme Mendel thought that one over. "All right," he said to Malone, "all right. Right now I can't do anything but believe you. But I'll say this much. Even if you don't know where she is, I believe you can find her. And if you don't deliver her to me in twenty-four hours, I'll have you put in jail for obstructing justice."

"Go right ahead," said Malone nastily, "and I'll get myself out of there so fast it'll make your ears pop."

Mendel thought that one over too, decided to change the subject. "Miss Brand, there's something I want to ask you, too."

"If it's did I murder Aunt Alex, no, I didn't," she told him.

"I didn't say you did. I just want to know what you were doing here at the Inglehart house that night."

"I came over to return a scarf I'd borrowed from Holly," she said promptly. Too promptly, Jake thought.

"Why didn't you say something about it before?"

"Nobody asked me."

"You've been concealing evidence," Hyme Mendel told her irritably. "That's what you've been doing. The woman next door told me she saw you driving in here before midnight. You were here and you didn't say a word about it. I could arrest you for it."

Hyme Mendel would feel a great deal happier if he could just arrest somebody, Jake decided.

"I didn't think it was important," Helene said. "I was only here for a minute. In fact, I hadn't even remembered it until now."

"Was Mrs. Dayton here then?"

"She was," Helene said. "She was in bed, just going to sleep."

"But God damn it, she couldn't have been," exploded the district attorney.

"But God damn it, she was," Helene said coolly.

"Miss Brand," said Mr. Fleck miserably, "you hadn't ought to use language like that."

Nobody paid any attention to him.

"All right," said Hyme Mendel furiously, "all right. I can't get anything out of any of you. But if Mrs. Dayton isn't turned over to me in twenty-four hours, there's going to be hell popping."

Malone looked at him coldly. "She will be."

Mendel stood up, fastened his overcoat, spun his derby by the brim a few times, dropped it, blushed, picked it up, mentally kicked himself. "She'd better be."

He led the unhappy Jasper Fleck out of the room. A moment later they heard the front door close.

Jake looked at Helene. "Now will you tell me," he began in an ominous voice.

Just at that moment the Parkins' alarm clock took it upon itself to ring, long, loud, blatantly, and enthusiastically.

It was the last straw.

Helene hopped off the hen's nest of clocks, fell into a chair, and collapsed into a state of shrieking hysteria.

Jake shook her into silence. "A thread of your coat got tangled up with the alarm release and set the alarm going."

"If it had happened while they were here!" Helene gasped.

"Well, it didn't."

She drew a long breath. "We," she said, "are the three most absent-minded people this side of heaven."

Jake stared at her.

"The alarm clocks," Helene said. "Where are the alarm clocks Holly heard that night?"

He continued to stare at her.

"Assuming," she continued, "that she really did hear alarm clocks ringing."

"If she says she heard them, she did," Jake said. "But where? Why?"

"Don't ask me why. Don't ask why about any of this or you'll tempt me into saying something unnecessarily rude. As for where—" She shrugged her shoulders. "She heard one ringing in Glen's room. When she got there, it had stopped. Then one began to ring in the Parkins' room—but not the Parkins' clock."

"Obviously not the Parkins' clock," Malone said.

"And then one rang in Aunt Alex's room. Where were those clocks hidden?"

"They must have been hidden," Jake began.

"Of course. If they hadn't been, she would have seen them. Remember, she was clock-minded that night. If they hadn't been hidden, the police would have found them when they got here. Simple process of reason."

"Don't ever get beyond the simple processes," Jake implored, "you leave me winded."

She ignored him. "Malone, where are those clocks?"

"I don't know."

"Look here," Jake said, "the morning after the murder, the police really searched this house. Andy Ahearn may be dumb, but he's thorough. If those alarm clocks had been here, they would have been found—no matter how well they were hidden."

"But," she said, "but you believe that she heard them."

"Has it occurred to you," he inquired calmly, "that whoever hid them has probably had ample opportunity to take them away again?"

She looked at him thoughtfully. "That's what must have happened. But where are they now?"

"Probably at the bottom of the lake," Malone said.

She sighed. "Well—listen. No one would ordinarily own three alarm clocks. If we could find where someone had bought three alarm clocks—a clerk would notice anyone buying three of them at a time."

"Have you any idea," Malone asked icily, "how many stores sell alarm clocks? And have you thought that whoever bought the clocks thought of the same reaction on the part of the clerk and bought one alarm clock in each of three stores?"

"We could find out all the people who bought alarm clocks in any stores lately and see if any one of them was connected with the case."

Jake groaned. "You do everything the hard way."

"Do you know an easier one?"

"Find who had an opportunity to murder Alexandria Inglehart in the time between when Glen and Parkins left—when she was alive, and the time Holly walked into her room and found her dead, and among those people find one who had a motive to murder her—"

"And you say *I* do everything the hard way," Helene commented.

"In the meantime," Malone said, "shut up, and we'll go talk to Parkins."

Parkins was discovered in the butler's pantry, industriously polishing silver. His face was white and drawn; there were deep shadows under his eyes. Jake felt a sudden rush of sympathy for him.

"We want to talk to you," Malone said.

Parkins nodded without surprise. "Yes, sir. I'd rather expected it, sir, if I may say so." He wiped his hands carefully on a towel and led the way into the kitchen. "If you don't mind coming out here—"

"Not at all," Helene said, "it's the only cheerful room in the house."

"Now," said Malone. "Where did you go after you talked to Mr. Justus last night?"

"Go, sir?"

"Did you go back to the summerhouse?"

"Oh no, sir. After my encounter with Mr. Justus, I had an intimation that it might not be wise."

"Were you here all evening?"

"No, sir. I went out a little before nine."

Nine, Jake thought. It had been about nine when he had seen the dapper little dude going back to the summerhouse.

"Where did you go?"

"Well sir, Joe—the houseboy next door—asked me to run over and have a look at the oil burner. It wasn't working just right. So I repaired it for him, and a ticklish job it was, too. We were there till about ha' past ten, and then he came back with me for—" the little man coughed apologetically—"a bottle or so of beer."

"Did you leave the house after that?"

"Oh no, sir, Mr. Glen had a guest who stayed till quite late, and he kept me rather busy waiting on them."

"Who was the guest?"

"Mr. Mendel, sir. Mr. Hyme Mendel."

Malone showed no sign of surprise.

"He'd come here to question Glen?"

"Oh no, sir. It was more in the nature of a social call, sir. Mr. Glen had telephoned Mr. Mendel and asked him to drop in and discuss what progress had been made, and then they had a few drinks, and well, you know how those things are, sir."

"What time did he leave?"

"It was nearly three, sir."

"They were talking all that time?"

"No, sir. They were—ah—shooting craps, sir. Mr. Glen was complaining this morning that he'd, ah, lost his shirt."

Helene snickered.

"Where was Mrs. Parkins last night?" Malone asked.

"Mr. Glen gave her the night off, sir, and she left about seven to visit a sister in Oak Park."

Otherwise, Jake thought, Joe from next door would not have run over for a bottle or so of beer.

"What time did Mr. Mendel get here last night?"

"I really couldn't say for sure. Mr. Glen said he got here about nine o'clock. But I wasn't here to let him in. That was while I was next door."

"Do you usually repair the oil burner next door?"

Parkins nodded modestly. "I rather keep an eye on all of them in the neighborhood. I seem to have—well, something of a way with oil burners, sir."

"What was the matter with the one next door?"

An indignant light flared suddenly in Parkins' eyes. "Someone had been monkeying with it."

"Intentionally disabling it?"

"Yes, sir. Might have seriously injured it, too. Imagine anyone deliberately trying to damage a fine piece of machinery like that. Sheer vandalism, sir. It was a bit of a job to fix it, too. I told Joe they'd better be getting locks on the cellar windows. Anyone could get in and out as easy as butter."

"Any idea who might have damaged it?"

"None whatever, Mr. Malone." There was a sudden puzzled look in Parkins' mild gray eyes. "If I may ask, sir—"

The lawyer pounced on him suddenly. "You were on your way to the summerhouse when Mr. Justus stopped you last night?"

"Yes, sir. But after I—" Parkins stopped suddenly.

"It's all right, Parkins," Malone said soothingly. "You admitted it with the first words you spoke to me." He pounced again, looking straight at the little man. "Tell me the truth, Parkins. Who is he?"

Parkins hesitated a moment, gulped, and was irretrievably lost. "The father of Miss Holly and Mr. Glen, sir. That's who he is. Miss Holly and Mr. Glen's father."

CHAPTER 27

"His name is Lewis Miller," Parkins said. "I don't know where he comes from, but he's an actor. Not a very good one, I'd imagine."

"And he's the father of Glen and Holly?"

"Yes, sir."

"How do you know?"

"He told me so, sir."

"He could have been lying to you, you know," Malone said.

"Yes, Mr. Malone. I thought of that. But I know that he wasn't. Because he showed me letters Miss Alexandria wrote him at the time the twins were born."

Jake tried to make his mind stop whirling in dizzy circles. Where did the father of Holly and Glen fit into the insane picture?

"How long has he been living in the old summerhouse, Parkins?"

"Oh, several days, sir." He took a long breath and plunged into the whole story. "It was the day after the murder, sir. I was that upset about it, Mr. Malone, as you can well imagine. And it did seem to me, sir, though goodness only knows I wasn't the one to be saying so, that they were making a most terrible mistake in taking Miss Holly away to the jail. But you see, sir, it was either Miss Holly or Mr. Glen."

"Glen?" said Malone casually.

Parkins was suddenly silent and miserable.

"It's all right," Malone told him, "we know about Glen and your daughter Maybelle."

Parkins sniffed. "It was none of Mr. Glen's fault, sir. But Miss Alexandria always kept him cooped up here pretty close, and Maybelle, sir, for all she's my own child, has always been a headstrong girl and a downright wayward one."

Jake felt an ache of sympathy for Parkins, with Maybelle for a daughter and Nellie for a wife.

"But I knew it couldn't be either Miss Holly or Mr. Glen, sir, and so I knew it had to be someone else. Only I knew I couldn't convince anybody it was a mistake arresting Miss Holly, unless maybe I could find out who really murdered Miss Alexandria." He paused, seemed a trifle embarrassed. "I've always rather fancied, sir, that I should have made a fair detective, if I'd been started off differently as a boy. I'm a great reader of detective fiction, sir."

Lies there a man with soul so dead, Jake thought, who doesn't think he would have made a fair, or better than fair, detective!

"I quite understand, Parkins. Go on."

"Well sir, after things had quieted down a bit, so to speak, and after they had taken Miss Alexandria away, I started making a most careful examination of the house. But I didn't find anything worth while. I thought that perhaps if I could just find a coat button, sir, or something of the sort, it would give me a start. I did find a tiepin on the carpeting of the hall right outside the—the murder room, but it turned out to belong to Mr. Ahearn."

Jake could imagine the little man's disappointment.

"And then, sir, I concluded that I would extend my investigation to the grounds around the house. I went over them most minutely, Mr. Malone—for footprints especially. Only it had snowed that night, as you recall, and then so many people had been walking around and around the house, it was practically impossible to locate any footprints. Then I looked along the lake shore and while I was there I just happened to look into the old summerhouse."

Jake had a fleeting vision of Ambrose Parkins sniffing along the lake shore, finally reaching the summerhouse and peering in the window.

"You can readily imagine my astonishment, sir."

"We can," said Helene with feeling.

"Why didn't you tell the police?" Jake asked.

Ambrose Parkins all but blushed. "I wanted to make my discovery alone, sir. Of course I intended to tell the police everything, but not until I had discovered who murdered Miss Alexandria."

"I see. But why didn't you tell me or Mr. Justus?"

"I was afraid you might laugh at me, sir. So I decided to watch the summerhouse and see who entered it. It was a bit difficult, watching the summerhouse and tending to everything here at the same time, especially as Mrs. Parkins is a rather suspicious woman, sir. But I managed it, only I didn't see anyone in the summerhouse until night. Then I saw a bit of light through the window, not much light, but enough that I knew someone was there."

"And then?"

"Well sir, I put on my coat and muffler and went straight down there. I wasn't sure of what to do, but finally I decided the wisest method of procedure was to walk straight in and confront the fellow. And that, sir, is just what I did do."

"Were you armed?"

"Oh no, sir. Weapons of any kind have always made me extremely nervous."

"Go on," said Malone hoarsely.

Unarmed, Jake thought, and with the man in the summerhouse a probable murderer, Ambrose Parkins decides to walk straight in and confront the fellow!

"He was quite definitely surprised, sir, but he told me that he could explain everything. Then he showed me the letters Miss Alexandria had written him at the time the twins were born, and told me that he was their father. He told me that he knew who the real murderer was but that he couldn't prove it yet, and that I must help him and not hinder him, for Miss Holly's sake."

"How did you help him?"

"Just by letting him stay on in the summerhouse, and not telling a soul that he was there, not even Mr. Glen. And by keeping a bit of a fire there when he wanted it. Only he warned me not to come to the summerhouse until he told me to. So I was most careful not to."

Naturally, Jake thought. If Parkins had gone down to the summerhouse he would have discovered Dick—left there to die, or until the dapper man decided how to dispose of him.

"But you were going there last night anyway?"

"Yes, sir. I couldn't help myself. What with Miss Holly escaped from jail and disappeared and her nice young man disappeared and no one knowing where he was and poor Mr. Glen nearly sick with anxiety, I was quite beside myself, Mr. Malone. I was indeed. I felt that I had to find out what was happening and I couldn't think of anyone else who might know."

Malone put a hand on Parkins' shoulder. "Don't worry, Parkins. I can tell you one thing for certain. Miss Holly is alive and well and safe, and her husband is alive and well and safe."

"Oh, thank you, sir!" Parkins almost smiled.

Malone rose to his feet. "Well, I guess that's about all, Parkins. Except that I have a nasty little job of work for you to do."

"For me, sir?"

"Yes, Parkins. We're going back to the Brand garage. After you see us drive away, I want you to phone to the police—Mr. Fleck's office—and tell them there is somebody dead in the Inglehart summerhouse."

For just an instant Jake thought the little man was going to faint. Then he regained his professional composure.

"Dead, sir?" with only the faintest trace of polite sunrise.

"That's right, Parkins, dead. The man who's been staying there. Tell the police you saw lights there last night and decided today that you'd go down and investigate, and found the body."

"Yes, sir. Should I tell them anything more, sir?"

Malone actually smiled at him. "No, Parkins. Much better not. Don't tell them a damned thing."

"Very well, sir." It was as though he was receiving an order to serve Holandaise with the artichokes.

The three of them started back to the Brand garage.

"What time would you say the guy was killed?" Jake asked.

"I'm not a doctor, but I'd say roughly it was sometime before midnight."

"It wasn't before nine," Jake said, "because he wasn't there. That sets the time pretty well between nine and midnight."

"That lets out Glen and both the Parkinses, if Nellie really was at her sister's in Oak Park," Helene said.

"And Holly's out," Jake said, "we know where she was."

"I hope you do," Malone said.

"Leave Holly out of this," Jake said. "She's your client, damn you." He paused for thought. "It's a good thing it's been snowing all day, or the collection of footprints around that summerhouse would have the Blake County cops running hog-wild."

Butch met them at the door of the garage, his face wrinkled with anxiety.

"Say, that guy is gone."

"You don't mean Dick?"

"I sure as hell do mean Dick. I just left him alone for a minute and he's gone!"

CHAPTER 28

"For God's sake, give me a drink," Jake said hoarsely.

Helene found the bottle and handed it to him.

"Maybe," Butch said unhappily, "maybe I shouldn't of told him she was at Madam Fraser's."

"Oh," said Malone, "so that's where you've hidden her."

Jake and Helene looked at him, startled.

"You could pretend you didn't hear him," Helene said.

"It's all right now," Malone told her, mopping his face. "It's all right now."

"He's probably on his way there right now," Jake groaned.

"It's too late to stop him," Helene said consolingly. "We'll hope the cops don't pick him up on the way."

"With that photographed face of his, and with a bandage around his bean, he's no more conspicuous than you would be at a W. C. T. U. picnic," Jake said. "But there's nothing to do about it now."

"We'll bawl him out when we get there," Helene promised.

Jake sighed. "It's the noble streak in him coming out," he said. "I never saw such a musician in my life. That's what comes of being brought up by an old-maid aunt in Grove Falls, Iowa. He looks like a blond angel and he damn near is one."

"All this is very pretty," Malone growled, "but no help." He took a package of papers from his pocket. They were the papers he had taken from the pocket of Lewis Miller, the little dude. Jake and Helene eyed them curiously.

There were some unpaid bills, a suburban time-table, several letters written in violet ink, a yellowed newspaper clipping with a picture showing Lewis Miller doing a human-fly act in Pittsburgh, a folded document, and an empty envelope. Malone glanced through the lot; laid the last two aside.

"This is interesting," he said, pointing to the document. "It's the original agreement he signed and gave to Alexandria Inglehart in which, for the sum of fifteen thousand dollars, he agreed to relinquish any future claim on either of the two children."

"But how could he get hold of that agreement?" Jake asked.

"I have a pretty good idea. Helene, where would this have been kept?"

"In the safe in Aunt Alex's room," she said promptly.

Malone nodded. "That's why he was there on the night of the murder. He was doing a job of burglary."

They thought that over for a moment. Suddenly Jake remembered something.

"Malone! He said—'Do you want to know why the window was open? I opened it.' That's why the window was open!"

Malone nodded. "Holly said that when she went in the room, the safe was just slightly ajar. That's why. But—" he frowned, "Nellie Parkins and Glen both said that when they went in the safe was closed."

"Miller opened the safe," Helene murmured. "But who closed it?"

"Is it possible," Jake asked, "that there's still another person involved in this—someone we haven't discovered yet—and that person murdered the old woman, and closed the safe—and stopped the clocks, and made the beds, and Holly— Oh God," he said, "I'm going insane!"

"But," Malone said, "the old woman was dead when Miller went in via the window—unless he killed her himself—and in that case, why should this unknown make a second visit, to close the safe after Miller opened it?"

"I ask the questions," Jake said, "I don't answer them."

"What's the empty envelope?" Helene asked.

Malone handed it to her.

"Where's the letter?"

"Lost or destroyed, I suppose. It doesn't matter. The envelope is the item of interest to me."

They examined it. It was addressed to Lewis Miller, at a New York address. There was a name and return address on the back. The return address was that of Maybelle Parkins. But the name above it was that of Nellie Parkins.

"And it's her writing, too," Helene said slowly, "I recognize it."

"The postmark—" Jake said suddenly.

Malone nodded. "It was mailed nearly a week before the murder of Miss Inglehart. In other words, while we don't know what that letter said, the chances are that Nellie Parkins knew about the man in the summerhouse." In the pause that followed, Helene poured three drinks.

"I've got to have a drink," she said. "I need a clear head to think this over."

Malone was buttoning his overcoat.

"I'll drive you anywhere," Helene offered.

"You'll drive him anywhere," Malone said, pointing to Jake, "to drink, probably. But not me, you won't. Anyway, my car's out here."

"Where are you going now?" Jake asked.

"St. Louis," said Malone calmly, looking for his gloves and finding them in his brief case.

"Wait a minute, damn you. What do you expect to find there? What are you going to St. Louis for?"

He grinned at them. "The murderer of Alexandria Ingle-hart," he said, and started for the door. Suddenly he paused. "Forgot something. Helene, when the phone rings in the Ingle-hart house, can you hear it upstairs?"

She shook her head. "No. Damned inconvenient. Aunt Alex hated all telephones. So it was an especially soft bell that could hardly be heard outside the room."

"Thanks. That's all I wanted to know."

Before they could ask another question, he was gone.

Jake and Helene finished the bottle gloomily.

"St. Louis. I wonder why he's going there. I wonder if—" She stopped.

"Why? What's about St. Louis?"

"It's where Glen and Holly were born. It's where that agreement was signed. Damn the man. Why couldn't he tell us more?"

Jake sighed.

Suddenly there was the sound of footsteps coming up the stairs.

"Maybe he's coming back—" Jake said hopefully.

The door opened and Hyme Mendel walked into the room.

Helene greeted him cheerfully. "Sorry we can't offer you a drink."

"I'm afraid I couldn't accept it," Mendel said stiffly.

Jake looked up curiously. Had the murder of the man in the summerhouse been discovered? No, that was impossible. There would have been police cars, sirens. And Parkins was not to call the police till all of them had left the Brand garage.

Then he saw that Helene was suddenly pale.

"Miss Brand," said the young district attorney, "you've lied to me." He sounded as though it were a personal affront. "It was later than you led us to believe when you came back to the Inglehart house that night. I've just been talking to the woman who saw you."

Helene made no answer.

Hyme Mendel seemed deeply grieved. "It was late enough for you to have done the murder, in fact."

Jake glared at him. "What do you think you're doing?"

"I think I'm arresting Miss Brand." Mendel took a long breath. "I'm not arresting her on suspicion of homicide, but as a material witness. She's been concealing evidence, to say the least."

"You're just making a big play," Jake said indignantly. "The papers are riding your tail because you let Holly Dayton get out from under your nose, and you think by putting another suspect in the can you'll make the public think you're getting somewhere."

"Shut up," Hyme Mendel said, "or I'll take you along too."

"At least give her a chance to explain," Jake bawled at him.

"I wouldn't explain the first principles of arithmetic to him," Helene said nastily.

"Miss Brand—" Hyme Mendel began.

"You can't arrest me and you aren't taking me to any jail," Helene said in a surprisingly loud and clear voice. "Can you get that through your fat head? You ought to be back at your job delivering coats and pants from the cleaners. Someday somebody's going to take *you* to the cleaners. But if you think you can take me to jail, you're full of hop."

The district attorney turned white with rage.

"I *am* arresting you. Miss Brand—"

"You go to hell," Jake muttered.

Downstairs he could hear the roar of Helene's car being started.

"You keep out of this," Hyme Mendel said to Jake. "She's coming along with me." He laid a hand on Helene's arm. Helene slapped him with breathtaking swiftness.

It was too much for the harassed young lawyer. With a kind of growl, he grabbed at Helene's wrist. At that moment Jake sent home one quick, well-directed punch that came all the way form his heels.

Hyme Mendel, district attorney of Blake County, collapsed in a little heap at their feet.

Helene grasped Jake's arm, pulled him through the door and down the stairs. The big sleek car was waiting, half through the door, its motor running.

"I heard you talking, Miss Brand," Butch said joyously, as Helene slid into the driver's seat.

Before Jake could catch his breath, they were half-way through Maple Park.

"Butch knows how to plan a quick getaway," Helene said. "Well, I've always wanted to be a fugitive from justice."

"From Jake Justus?" he asked.

She laughed. "Why don't you find out?"

"If the cops catch up with you, I'll send you candy in jail," he promised her.

They abandoned the car in a side street in Evanston, where Helene said Butch could pick it up later, found a taxi, and drove to the little bar where Helene had conducted her experiment with the beer glasses. There they found a secluded booth and ordered rye.

Jake looked at her curiously.

"So you didn't do it, Helene," he said thoughtfully. "But you've been shielding somebody. Obviously, it was Glen. But in the first place, why do you think he did it, and in the second place, why do you care?"

CHAPTER 29

THERE WAS that look in her eyes, the one that he had seen that night at the hotel. It was a look that hurt.

"Go on," he said hoarsely, "tell me."

"Don't you see," she began helplessly.

"Tell me!"

"It was either Glen or Holly. I knew it was one of them. I didn't know which, and I don't know now. But—don't you see?" she said again. "Whichever one it was—"

He tried to look at her calmly. "Did you make two trips to the Inglehart house that night?"

She nodded slowly. "Yes, I did."

"Then why in the name of God haven't you told us?"

"Because—" she hesitated a moment. "It made it look worse for Holly."

"What are you talking about, or do you know?"

"I went back that second time," she said slowly, "because I was worried about Holly. When I was there the first time she seemed—well, strange. I told you that."

"Yes. But the second time—"

"I had a few drinks and drove around Maple Park, and finally decided to go back and see if she was all right. That was when

I skidded and drove across a corner of the next-door lawn. The house was all dark but I let myself in—I had a key Nellie'd given me years ago—and went up to Holly's room." She paused.

"Well—what?"

"She wasn't there. Her bed hadn't been slept in."

Jake sat staring at her for a long moment. "What time was it?" he said at last.

"It was sometime around eleven. I don't know exactly."

"What did you do then?"

"Well, I—stood there a minute wondering what to do. I remembered what Holly had told me about her affair with Dick Dayton, and I wondered if she'd run away with him. But her bed's being made puzzled me. So I thought I'd wake up Glen. I went out into the hall and there was Glen, coming down the hall."

"He knew you'd made that second trip to the house?"

She nodded again. "I told him—or started to tell him—about Holly—and he told me about the telephone call. He was just getting ready to leave. I offered to go with him—drive him to the hospital—but he said Parkins was getting the car out, and I wouldn't be any help. So I left. Afterward I thought it was funny Holly could have gotten far enough south to have been in an accident near St. Luke's Hospital in the time since I'd made my first visit—when she certainly was getting into bed and asleep. But I told you I was a little hazy about the time."

Jake frowned. "At a little after eleven, she was gone and her bed wasn't slept in. You and Parkins and Glen swear to that. But at three o'clock or after—oh hell no, we don't know what time it was—well anyway, she woke up in her bed with no recollection of being out of it. And then when Nellie Parkins came home, Holly's bed hadn't been slept in. Somebody is crazy."

"You can see why I had to keep still about it," she said defensively, "because it simply made it look worse for her." She scowled. "Or Glen. The trouble is—he couldn't have gotten back to the house and done the murder after they left because he was with Nellie and Parkins all the time. But— couldn't he have—" She paused again.

"Look, Jake. When they came back from the hospital— couldn't he have done it—before Nellie and Parkins came into the room? Oh no, because of Holly. Holly discovered the murder before they came back. Unless the whole thing was a cockeyed telepathic dream Holly had."

"You'd better have another drink," he told her.

"The best thought you've had since we've been in here."

"Anyway," he reminded her, "it was Nellie who went in the room first, not Glen. But you've believed it was Glen who killed the old woman, haven't you?"

"Yes."

"But of all the people we've considered—Glen has no motive at all. You can't expect me to believe that he ever intended to marry Maybelle Parkins. Is that your theory? That—" He thought a moment. "Glen was going to marry Maybelle, and Auntie found it out, and it was Glen she was going to disinherit, not Holly—nuts. I can't see Glen marrying that floozie, especially if he was going to be kicked out of his aunt's will for it."

"It wasn't Maybelle Glen wanted to marry," Helene said in a strange voice. "It was me."

He wondered audibly and profanely if his ears were deceiving him.

"He asked me to marry him. I said I would. God knows why. Oh, I'd grown up with Glen and I liked him as well as anybody in the world, and I didn't have anybody else I wanted to marry, and I certainly didn't want to end up a society old maid with a paid companion, and Glen and I liked going to the same parties, which is all it takes for a successful marriage anyway, so I said I would. He asked me for the same reasons. Holly and Glen and I were always pretty close to each other, but that was all. He didn't make much fuss when the idea was given up."

"Why was it given up?" Jake asked as casually as he could.

"Because of Aunt Alex. She was pretty damn fussy about who marries an Inglehart. And I'd gotten into a fairly sordid mess once in my impetuous way and only the grace of God and my old man's money saved me from a nasty scandal. Aunt Alex found out all the dope on it and somehow managed to corral all the letters that had been written back and forth. Probably knew she'd have use for them. So when Glen brought up the subject of marrying me, she called me in for a conference and told me to lay off Glen. She had the letters in her safe and told me she'd make no bones about using them if I hinted at marrying her nephew."

Jake wondered vaguely what the fairly sordid mess had been. "How did Glen take it?"

"He didn't know anything about it. I just told him I'd changed my mind. I don't think he ever found out the reason unless—"

"Unless he found out the real reason and murdered the old dame because of it?"

She nodded.

"Where are the letters now?"

"Mr. Featherstone found them in the safe the day after the murder, and sent them to me with a note of apology for reading them. I don't think he needed to apologize."

"Why not?"

"I don't think he understood them. Anyway they're burned now."

"Glen found out about it and murdered the old woman to save you, his boyhood chum, from trouble. Pretty thin. If he'd done that he'd have removed the letters himself while he had the chance. Glen didn't find out about it and decided he wanted to marry you in spite of Auntie's opposition, and did her in to get the opposition out of the way. Pretty thin. She was going to die anyway in a few months. Glen wanted to marry Maybelle Parkins in spite of her taste in decoration, and murdered Auntie so he could do it. Pretty thin. Same reason as above." He looked at her. "Still believe Glen did it?"

"I don't know what to believe."

He spread out his fingers and began counting on them. "First, must consider motives. One doesn't ordinarily murder an old woman who is going to die in a few months anyway. Not unless there is a particular reason why she had to die at a particular time. In this case, there was. She was going to change her will the next day. If we knew who she was going to disinherit the next day, we'd know who murdered her. Maybe."

"You mean we'd know if it was Glen or Holly."

"Exactly. But damn it to hell, it couldn't have been either of them. She was alive when Glen left the house and dead when he came back, and we know where he was all the time in between. And Holly—well, her story is the truth, or I'm a Chinaman."

"Are you going to open a laundry, or just go fight the Japanese?" she inquired.

"Shut up. There might have been another reason why she had to die that night. She might have known something and been planning to use it."

"What do you mean?"

He looked at her closely.

"Now that I think of it, why were you so damned anxious to spring Holly from the Blake County can?"

"I told you why at the time."

"Did you? Helene, it couldn't have been because you didn't want your childhood playmate to take the rap, was it?"

In the half darkness her face suddenly grew white, pointed. Her great eyes became wary and foxlike.

"You could have done it so easily. You've even told me why. You weren't shielding Glen, you were shielding yourself. You could have imitated Holly's voice."

"There's something in my mind that I don't quite like," she said.

"There's something in my mind that I don't quite like either," he told her.

She stared at him. "Well, why don't you do something about it? Tell Malone. Tell Hyme Mendel, he'd love it. Or just call a cop. Or shall I call one?"

"Oh damn you, Helene, you know I can't do that."

"Startling development in Maple Park murder," she chanted. "North-shore debutante confesses. Read Helene Brand's own story of the crime on page three."

"Stop that, Helene, stop that. I can't stand much more."

"What are you going to do about it?"

"Do?" He stared at her. "Oh God, I can't do anything. I can't do a damned thing, except go on thinking about it, forever, perhaps. And let Holly live her life out with everyone in the world, except you and me, believing she's a murderess. Helene, I can't do anything."

"You wouldn't turn me in?"

"Not even for Holly's sake."

Suddenly she smiled. "While you're thinking about it, you might figure Lewis from St. Louis into your calculations and maybe you won't be so sure I'm a murderess from Maple Park."

He blinked.

"And add in why Malone is going to St. Louis and why the little dude was getting letters from Nellie Parkins, and why he was murdered, and why someone stopped all the clocks at three."

"Helene— "

"I can't answer any of them, but maybe Malone will."

"Oh God," he said, "Helene, forgive me."

Suddenly she was in his arms. Her elbow knocked over the glass of rye.

"I'll buy you another one," he promised.

"Two other ones?"

"Two."

"Then I'll forgive you."

The bartender came and wiped the table disapprovingly.

"Look, Jake. Holly's pa is down-and-out. Broke. And his children are rolling in luxury. It irks him. He needs money. You follow me?"

"I could do better with a map."

"Well, anyway, he comes here. Knows he can't get any more dough out of Aunt Alex. So he figures that he'll bump off the old lady, get back that agreement he signed years ago and burn it, and then, with Aunt Alex safely buried, he'll turn up as the long-lost papa and his affectionate children will support him the rest of his natural life."

"A very pretty theory," Jake said, "and interesting, too."

"It might even be correct."

"Where," said Jake wearily, "was Holly all this time?"

"She was there and she knows who did it, and she's telling this fantastic story and refusing to tell the truth because he's her father."

"Who stopped the clocks?" Jake asked, "and why were they all stopped at three? And how about the beds being made?"

"Those problems," she told him firmly, "are out of my department."

"And if that's how it happened," Jake went on, "why is Malone going to St. Louis and why did he ask that about the telephone?"

"He could be making an error, you know."

"Not Malone."

Helene sighed.

"And finally," Jake said, "if the long-lost papa killed Alexandria Inglehart, who killed *him?*"

"His conscience began to bother him and he committed suicide," Helene suggested hopefully.

"Stabbing himself three times to do it," Jake said in disgust, "the last two times after he was dead."

"Well anyway," she said, "it was a good idea as far as it went."

"It didn't go far enough," Jake told her. "That was its only fault."

A newsboy strolled through the bar. Jake bought a paper.

"Fast work," he said admiringly.

The story of the murder of an unidentified man in the Inglehart summerhouse was already screaming from the headlines.

SECOND CLOCK KILLING STIRS MAPLE PARK

HUNT HOLLY AND DICK AFTER NEW SLAYING

"Even while police of three states searched last night for Holly Inglehart Dayton, missing Maple Park murderess, and her husband Dick Dayton, famous band leader, an unidentified man was slain in the old summerhouse of the Inglehart estate. Police believe that the missing girl returned, eluding their—"

"Oh God," said Helene, "of course they credit Holly with this."

"Naturally," Jake told her. "Now if she'd been parked safely in the Blake County jail, they'd know damned well she couldn't have done this murder, and they might begin to wonder if she'd done the first one. But as it is—"

"Shut up," she told him indignantly. "You thought it was a good idea yourself."

"At the time," Jake said.

"Still," Helene said, "she's pretty well alibied at Madam Fraser's. We know she was there all the time and we can probably prove it."

"We hope," said Jake piously. He kissed her enthusiastically. "I can think of better things to do, but perhaps we'd better get on our horses and get to the Fraser castle. After all," he said, grinning at the memory of Hyme Mendel's startled face, "after all, baby, she's not the only one who needs a hide-out now!"

CHAPTER 30

JAKE AND Helene hailed a taxi at the corner, gave the driver an address about a block from the Fraser house.

"Hope Dick got there all right," Jake muttered.

Halfway to their destination they stopped and bought another paper. An unflattering portrait of Helene adorned the front page.

POLICE HUNT BRAND HEIRESS

IN MAPLE PARK MURDERS

"It must be wonderful to be famous," Jake murmured.

The driver heard him and turned around. "That girl on the front page is a looker all right," he said.

"Oh I don't know," Jake said, squinting at the picture.

The driver grinned. "Well, I wouldn't mind a chance to get acquainted with her."

"If you ask me," Helene said, "I think she looks like a dope."

"Who do you think is doing all those murders?" the driver asked chummily over his shoulder.

"Confidentially," Jake said, "it looks like a gangland killing to me."

Another headline caught his eye.

BLAKE COUNTY D.A. BRUTALLY ASSAULTED

"It must be wonderful to be brutal," Helene murmured very softly. "But I'd never dreamed you really were."

"Would you like to find out?" Jake asked pleasantly.

Jasper Fleck had voiced an opinion to an American reporter that Maple Park was having a crime wave. The search for Holly Inglehart Dayton was being pressed, after the second murder on the Inglehart estate. Pictures of Holly, Dick, Glen, and the summerhouse were plastered across the second page. Hyme Mendel was deeply chagrined that a murder had been committed in the Inglehart summerhouse while he was "conversing," as the papers expressed it, with Glen in the Inglehart library.

The radio column was devoted largely to a description of Dick Dayton's band carrying on in the absence of the leader. On the front page of the second section a well-known woman reporter discussed: "Where are Holly and Dick," and painted a gloomy picture of the escaped pair spending their lives in hiding and living to a miserable and conscience-stricken old age in some obscure and distant hamlet.

And no one had been able to identify the little man found dead in the summerhouse.

At Madam Fraser's they found Dick and Holly cozily holding hands, talking with their hostess, and surrounded by photographs.

"And here she is at fifteen," Mrs. Fraser was saying. "That's the year she was honor student in her class." She looked up and beamed. "Good afternoon, Miss Brand and Mr. Justus. I've just been showing some photographs of Jane."

She collected the photographs and left them after a moment's conversation.

Jake had forgotten all he had planned to say to Dick for running away from them. Dick, it appeared, had already told Holly his adventure, and of the murder of the man in the summerhouse.

"And nobody knows who he is," Holly mused.

"The police don't know," Jake said, "but we know. Malone knows."

"*Who* is he?"

"Your father," Helene spoke quickly.

Jake told the rest of the story then, while Holly and Dick stared at him.

"But why did Malone ask that about the telephone?" Holly asked.

"I don't know," Jake said. "I don't know, but it bothers me. And this trip to St. Louis bothers me. I'm not sure why, but it does."

"Me, too," Helene confessed.

"It involves you a little too much, somehow," Jake told Holly. "I'm not positive how, but it does. For one thing, because you were born in St. Louis. Then there was that agreement we found in—in your father's pocket. No, you're involved in this somehow, and I don't know exactly how you are, and it bothers me."

"I wish we knew," Holly sighed.

"I'm afraid we will know, when Malone gets back from his trip to St. Louis," Helene said.

"Afraid?" Holly repeated.

"Holly, please try to think," Helene said imploringly, with almost desperation in her voice, "why would your father have wanted to get back that agreement?"

"I don't know."

"Don't you know anything about him?"

"No, not anything. I just assumed somehow that he was dead. I don't remember ever seeing him, never in my whole life."

"Holly, try to remember."

"Don't bully her, Helene," Jake said.

"I'm trying to help her, you fool. She's in danger, whether you realize it or not. Here, Holly, take a drink, a stiff one. I don't care if Ma Fraser does disapprove."

"All right. Thanks."

"Listen, Holly. Try to think. There was so much happening those last few days before the murder. You were all tired-out and nervous and upset. There was a lot worrying you."

"You talk just like John J. Malone," Jake murmured.

"Are you trying to make out that she lost her mind?" Dick said crossly.

"Oh God, no. Nothing like that. But people have lapses. Holly, you might have forgotten. Maybe that's what you can't remember. Your father—"

"I meet a father that I haven't seen since I was a baby and talk with him, and it's such a faint little triviality that it slips my mind," said Holly indignantly.

"I don't mean that kind of forgetting. Nothing like it. Holly, he was in the house during those hours when you can't remember what happened. We know that. And we know you can't remember what happened then. We don't even know where you were."

"It's possible," Holly said slowly.

"Helene, what are you trying to do?" Dick said desperately.

"Holly"—paying no attention to him—"Holly, when I saw you that night, when you were just getting into bed, there was something strange about you. I don't know what it was, but I noticed it even then. You weren't like yourself at all."

"I know it," the red-haired girl answered. "I can remember that. I remember your being there, but terribly dimly. Everything is hazy and—oh, all mixed up."

"There. You see? The only thing you do know is that you were asleep all that time—or rather you think that you were asleep right there in bed. But we know you weren't in bed. *Where were you?*"

"I don't know. That's just it. I don't know."

"Helene, let her alone," Dick said.

"Shut up, you. I've got to make her think. Holly, you were somewhere else. But where? Where were you? During that time you might have met and talked with your father. People's minds do have lapses like that. You might have gone anywhere, done anything —"

"I might," said Holly very slowly, "I might have lured Glen and Parkins away from the house and murdered Aunt Alex."

"No," said Jake Justus, "it didn't happen that way."

"*But Malone thinks it did!*" Helene said desperately.

They stared at her in blank amazement.

"Don't be a complete idiot," said Jake but he could not make himself say it convincingly.

"See. You think so too, but you won't admit it."

"But *why*, Helene?" Holly asked, white-faced.

"I'm sure of it. He knows that this murder is tied up with Holly in some manner, and right now, right this minute, he's finding out how. It ties up somehow with you and your father, and that's why he's gone to St. Louis. Holly, don't you remember, your father told us *he* was the motive for the murder."

"Why not Glen as much as Holly?" Jake asked.

"It could be. But Holly is the one involved in this. Look—" She faced him suddenly, eyes blazing. "Parkins is mixed up in this. He knows about the man in the summerhouse. Nellie is mixed up in it. We know that she wrote to this guy before he came to Chicago. We don't know why, but we know she did. This—this mystery—*may* concern Glen as much as Holly—"

"Then why pick on Holly?" Dick asked. "Why not Glen?"

"Because," Helene said, "Aunt Alex was murdered while Glen and Nellie and Parkins were driving down to the Loop. Unless all three of them, and Maybelle Parkins, and the attendant at St. Luke's Hospital are lying, they must have been. That leaves only two people on the scene—Holly and her father. That's what Malone knows."

"Then—but—Malone is supposed to be helping me," Holly said.

Jake nodded thoughtfully. "He was. But we accidentally put him on the spot by getting you out of the jug, Holly. He doesn't want to have it turn out this way. But he can't help himself. He's got to turn up a murderer—you or someone else—for Blake County, or be in the soup."

"Holly, listen," Helene begged, "you—"

She was interrupted by the arrival of Mrs. Fraser.

"There's the rye you ordered," said the lady sternly, "and there's the soda. And I suppose, your nerves being what they are, it's all right, and I admit this poor girl has been under a terrible strain, but just the same—" She set the tray down with a bang. "And another thing, Jake Justus. I wish you'd warn her not to go out of the house at night. It isn't safe. Someone's likely to see her and recognize her. And anyway this neighborhood is no place for her to be walking alone."

Jake turned to Holly with a frown. "Have you been out of the house?"

She nodded apologetically. "Only once. That was last night. I know that I shouldn't. But I'd been cooped up so long, and I wanted some fresh air, and I wanted to walk a little. I wore a veil and I stayed away from people, and nobody could have seen or recognized me."

Jake sighed. "Well, don't do it again. Where did you walk?"

"In Lincoln Park."

Mrs. Fraser beamed at her. "It's just that I don't want to see you took back to that jail again, dearie. I've grown real fond of you these past few days." She smiled at them all and went away.

Helene was staring at Holly, a puzzled look on her face. "Holly, how long were you out walking—what time was it?"

"Oh, I don't know exactly. I went out about ten o'clock, I guess, and I was gone about two hours."

"Oh God, Holly!"

"Why?"

"I see," said Jake. "Last night's murder was committed between nine and twelve, or thereabouts."

Holly turned white. "And you think that *I*—"

"Blake County will," said Jake gloomily. "In fact, Blake County already does."

"Look," Helene said, "we've got to get you away from here."

"What do you mean? Why?"

"Before it's too late. I'm afraid of what Malone is finding out. I'm afraid of what he has already found out. Holly, we'll cut your hair and dye it, and do some things with make-up, and I'll have Butch buy a good fast car and you can head for Mexico—"

"Of all the mad schemes—" Dick said.

"It isn't mad. It's the only thing to do. You don't want her to spend the rest of her life in the jug, do you?"

"We never could get away with it," Holly said.

"It's worth trying. It's worth taking the chance."

"You're right," Dick said after a while. "It's worth anything, Holly, to have you safe."

"I'd hate to see Holly spending her life as a fugitive from justice," Jake said thoughtfully. "I'd rather see her go through the worst of this and come out completely vindicated."

"But she wouldn't be," Helene said urgently.

Dick had seized on the idea. "We'll need money. The banks are closed. Where could we get that much cash at an hour like this?"

"You forget," Helene said, "I'm still carrying around the grand that we were going to give Holly's father this morning."

"Then that settles it," Dick said.

Jake looked at him. "Does it? Where do you fit into this picture? Holly won't be any nearer you in Mexico than she would be in jail."

"After things have quieted down a little, I could quietly slip away and join her there."

"But the band!" Jake howled.

"The hell with the band. Do you think anything is more important than Holly?"

They argued about it through dinner, through most of the evening. They beat Jake down to muttered instead of shouted "noes."

Helene tucked Dick's bandage under his hat, darkened his eyebrows and what showed of his hair with her eyebrow pencil.

"There. That ought to do it. Now—get Butch on the phone, from a corner drugstore. Have him meet you. Give him this—"

she stuck the envelope of money in his hand, "and tell him to get the fastest small car he can find, and bring it here. And have him bring a bottle of hair dye. Any color but red."

"And then?" Dick said.

"Well, then get in touch with Glen. We can trust him. Between you, you and Glen ought to be able to keep Hyme Mendel and the Blake County police involved in enough of a wild-goose chase out in Maple Park to give Holly more than an even chance."

"I'll do my best," Dick promised.

"Oh Dick," Holly wailed, "I won't see you now till God knows when!"

"It won't be long," Dick said. "It won't be long. And we have a whole lifetime."

They said good-by unhappily.

"Helene, I can't do this," Holly said, after he had gone.

"Don't be a sap. Do you want to spend the rest of your life having Dick coming to see you on visiting days? Sewing buttons on denim overalls? Perhaps being paroled after twenty years or so—half a lifetime off for good behavior—"

"Helene, please!"

"—Or wouldn't you rather say good-by to Dick like this, for a little while, than to tell him good-by the night before they electrocute you—"

"Damn you, shut up!" Jake said.

"It's all right," Holly said dully, "I'll do it."

"Good girl."

They finished the bottle of rye to celebrate Holly's decision. At last Helene borrowed scissors from Mrs. Fraser, wrapped a towel around Holly's shoulders and prepared to cut off the blazing glory of red hair.

There was a knock at the door.

"Probably the hair dye," Helene said, and called, "Come in."

It was not the hair dye. It was John J. Malone, very pale, very tired, and extremely untidy.

They stared at him. Helene dropped the scissors.

"How did you get here so fast?" Jake asked stupidly, for want of anything better to say.

"Flew," said Malone laconically. "Found out just what I wanted to know. Didn't need to find it out, either, after I realized what I did about Holly's voice."

"What about Holly's voice?" Helene asked.

"About its being imitated over the phone. It took me a long time to get it through my head, but finally I realized there was only one person who could have imitated Holly over the telephone."

"*Who?*"

"Holly herself," Malone said very calmly.

"Look here," Jake began furiously.

Malone ignored him. He regarded Holly thoughtfully. "I know just what you have in mind, but you'll have to get it out of your mind."

"What do you mean?" Helene asked.

He ignored her too. "Holly Dayton—I promised Hyme Mendel that I'd deliver you to him at your home, in just an hour from now. We'd better get going. The roads are bad between here and Maple Park."

CHAPTER 31

"Look here," said Jake, jumping up. "Look here, damn you. You can't do this, Malone."

Malone regarded him coldly and silently.

Helene's eyes were blue fire. "And I thought we could trust you."

"Apparently you were mistaken," Malone said. His voice sounded very tired.

"You're not taking her anywhere," Jake said. "You're not taking her to one damned place."

Malone slipped one hand ominously in his coat pocket. "Don't try to stop me, Jake. I'd hate to have trouble with you."

"You're going to have trouble if you try to get away with this. You can't do it. By God," he said bitterly. "I never thought I'd see my own lawyer pull a gun on me."

Malone turned to Holly.

"Are you ready?"

She regarded him for a moment, her eyes expressionless, her face very white.

"Yes, I am. I'm putting myself in your hands."

"Good." He turned to Jake and Helene. "You might do as much."

"How can we?" Helene asked. "How can we, after this?"

He shrugged his shoulders. "All right then. Mrs. Dayton, we'd better be on our way."

"I'm quite ready to go."

Jake remembered how she had used those same words, that morning in the Inglehart library.

"Holly!" Helene said desperately.

"It's all right, Helene."

She had said that, too. The whole thing seemed to be repeating itself, incredibly and horribly, with Malone in the place of Andy Ahearn.

"But Holly, you can't give up like this," Helene begged.

"It's the only thing I can do, now," Holly said. She took a coat from the closet and put it on.

They said good-by to Mrs. Fraser and went into the back-yard. At the entrance to the alley there was a patch of mud and melted snow. After a glance at it, Jake swung Helene into the waiting car, then Holly. As he lifted Holly, she gave a sudden moan.

"What's the matter?"

"There's a bruise there, under my arm—" She stopped suddenly. "A bruise—*Malone!*"

"What is it?"

"That's what I've been trying to remember. That's the thing I kept forgetting."

"*What are you talking about?*"

"In my dream. Remember? I was being hanged, and the rope kept slipping under my arms instead of around my neck. Remember?"

"Yes," said Malone.

"Then I woke up and felt so ill and strange and my flesh really was sore. I remember thinking it was strange a dream could be as real as that."

"And there's a mark there?"

Malone stared at her. "By God, that's it!"

"It's—what?"

"The one thing—the one more thing—I needed to know. Get in that car now and don't ask questions."

They drove to Maple Park in silence.

On the way, watching Helene, Jake began wondering again. Helene. In spite of everything. Oh damn it, why did he have to believe what he did?

Anyway, she couldn't have committed the second murder. She was asleep in the Brand garage and he was watching her. No, by God, he wasn't watching her all the time. He had gone to sleep, after he had seen the little dude go into the summerhouse. And Butch had been asleep. She could have slipped away without waking either of them, and slipped back again.

Would she tell the truth at the last minute and keep Malone from making this mistake?

And if she didn't, what would he do? Keep his mouth shut, and let them take Holly away to the jail again?

Would he ever be able to forget her?

The Inglehart house was a blaze of light. There were lights upstairs and downstairs; one shone brightly on the ugly old verandas. There was only one car in the driveway.

"Hyme Mendel promised not to bring too big an audience," Malone said. There was a curious, dreamlike quality about it all.

Glen met them at the door, his face white and set. "Helene, I couldn't help this. I tried—"

She paid little attention. "It's all right."

And there was Dick, very pale below his bandages.

"I did my best," he began unhappily.

"Forget it," Jake said.

Hyme Mendel, Jasper Fleck, and Andy Ahearn were waiting for them in the library.

"All set to make the pinch, eh?" said Malone with a little laugh.

Jake shuddered.

Hyme Mendel glared at them. "This is thoroughly illegal, Malone." Jake noticed a bruise on his jaw, inexpertly coated with pinkish powder. It was the one cheerful spot in the whole proceedings.

Jake looked around. For the first time they were all together—Holly, Dick, Helene, Glen, the Parkinses, even Maybelle. Malone sat down in the midst of the silent group; slowly and deliberately lit a cigar.

"I shall prove," he began in his best courtroom manner, "who murdered Miss Alexandria Inglehart in a room of this house four nights ago, and murdered a Mr. Lewis Miller in the summerhouse of the Inglehart estate last night, and I shall prove it in a manner that will leave no reasonable doubt in the minds of these gentlemen of the law, and even in the pigheaded mind of Jake Justus." He paused and cleared his throat.

"Miss Alexandria Inglehart was stabbed to death sometime during the night. The time has been set roughly between the hours of eleven and four."

Hyme Mendel looked up in sudden surprise.

Malone told him what they had discovered about the clocks.

"Now who would have thought of that," said Jasper Fleck admiringly.

Mendel glared at him.

"Mrs. Dayton, you were in bed at approximately ten o'clock?"

"Yes." It was only a breath.

"You can confirm that, Miss Brand?"

"I can," said Helene smoothly.

Malone nodded. "Mrs. Dalton, you remember nothing of what happened after you went to sleep until you woke, sometime in the night, and found yourself in your own bed?"

"Nothing. Except what I dreamed." Jake could see how tightly she was clutching Dick's hand.

"We'll come to the dream later," said Malone. He turned to Glen. "When you received the telephone call from your sister, you were in bed?"

"I was."

"You were in bed, too, Parkins?"

"Yes, sir," said the little man.

Again Malone nodded. "The beds, then, I take it, were mussed and rumpled. Yours too, Mrs. Dayton. But when your brother and the Parkinses came back to the house, all of the beds were smooth and neat, as though they had never been slept in."

Jake thought he heard Hyme Mendel sigh faintly.

"We'll get to that in a minute, too. First, about this telephone call." He looked at Holly for a moment. "Did you at any time during that night make a telephone call to anybody?"

"No."

"You are positive of that?"

"Yes."

"Good." Malone appeared to be thinking deeply for a moment. "Glen, you thought that you recognized your sister's voice?"

"I thought so, yes. If there was any difference, I probably put it down to the effect of the accident she said she had been in."

"I see."

"And besides," Glen finished, "I had been in bed and I just woke up. I probably wasn't paying much attention to what the voice sounded like. I was sleepy."

"Ah yes. You were in bed when the call came," said Malone thoughtfully.

"In bed and asleep."

"Parkins," Malone said casually, "it was Glen who answered the phone, not you?"

"That's right, sir."

"I thought so," Malone said. He looked at Glen. "In bed and asleep. Then tell me," he said in a suddenly thundering voice, "tell me, young man, how you heard the telephone ring, were awakened by it, when you were in bed and asleep and when the telephone cannot be heard ringing on the second floor of this house?"

Silence.

Then everyone started to speak at once.

"Shut up," said Malone calmly. "Parkins, what did you do after Mr. Glen told you of the call?"

"I dressed, sir, in something of a hurry, and I took one glance in Miss Holly's room to see if it was all ready for her. Then I went out and got the car. I had a bit of trouble getting it started, and then I drove it up to the house and picked up Mr. Glen."

"We've been assuming," said Malone slowly, "first, that Alexandria Inglehart was murdered at three o'clock, then, that she was murdered between the time when Glen and Parkins left the house and the time when they returned." He paused, and mopped his face with a crumpled and grayish handkerchief. "Parkins, when you drove away from the house, Alexandria Inglehart was still alive?"

"Yes, sir."

"How do you know? Did you go into her room?"

"No, sir. But I saw her sitting up in front of her window—" His voice broke suddenly and trailed away.

"Exactly," said Malone. "She was sitting up in front of the window when you found her dead, four hours later."

Again everyone started to speak at once. Malone waved them to silence.

"But sir," said Parkins, "the window was closed when we left, and it was open when Miss Holly went in there."

"Of course," said Malone, "we have only Holly's word for it that she didn't open it herself. But we're pretty sure that Alexandria Inglehart's body was left by that open window for some time."

Andy Ahearn nodded and cleared his throat. "Old lady was froze stiffer'n aboard."

"But how was the window opened?" Hyme Mendel asked.

"It was opened," said Malone, "by that same Lewis Miller who was found murdered in the Inglehart summerhouse last night. The same Lewis Miller who was Holly's father."

Hyme Mendel seemed too stunned for speech.

"And Glen's," Holly added.

"No," said Malone, shaking his head. "No. Not Glen's."

"But he's my brother. We're twins."

"No," said Malone again, "Glen is not your brother. You are not twins."

No one spoke.

Nellie Parkins, sitting up as straight as a ramrod, had been pale. Now she turned a pasty gray. Suddenly she seemed to collapse as though her bones had been turned to jelly, slipped sideways, and slid down to the floor.

Malone looked at her compassionately. "Someone take her away. Miss Parkins, you'd better go with her."

Andy Ahearn carried her, flopping against him like a disjointed doll, into the next room, Maybelle trailing after him. As though it seemed very important indeed at the time, Jake noticed that she did have run-over heels.

"I suggest," said Malone in the terrible silence, "that Alexandria Inglehart was already dead when Glen woke Parkins and told him about the telephone call that was never made. I suggest that the clocks in this house were set at three and stopped before Parkins ever woke—all save Parkins' own clock and that one was stopped while Parkins was getting the car. I suggest that during the time Parkins was getting the car, Glen's and Parkins' beds were made, and Holly Inglehart Dayton was put back in her bed from where—"

Jake never knew what really did happen. There was a sudden quick movement in the other end of the room; the lights went out. In the darkness he heard running feet, a table overturned, a door banged and locked.

Almost without thinking, he threw open one of the long French windows that opened onto the terrace, and ran out into the snow. In the distance he could see a black figure headed for the lake shore.

Instinctively, hardly knowing what he was doing, he ran after it.

CHAPTER 32

BEHIND HIM was the house, a blaze of lights. Dimly he could hear voices and shouts of confusion. Ahead of him was the lake shore and the cliff, with that treacherous sudden bluff, and the cruel jagged rocks below. Between him and the cliff was that running figure.

"Why am I doing this?" he wondered as he ran through the snow.

The figure grew nearer; he was gaining on it. He drew in his breath; ran a little faster.

If only he could make it before the figure reached the cliff.

What was the fool trying to do? Escape? Or was it suicide?

He was nearly at the cliff's edge. He could hear the water pounding against the stones and the broken cakes of ice that ground against the rocks.

He wasn't going over the cliff. He was going along the edge, making for the woods. Had a car hidden there, most likely. Probably been anticipating this.

Why not let him go? Perhaps he could get away safely. Spare Helene the agony of going through the trial, having the whole thing dragged on and on.

He kept on running.

Let him get away. Perhaps Helene actually cared for him. Nobody could tell what she actually thought or felt about anything. Let him get away, and then some day Helene would meet him somewhere and marry him.

The running figure was almost within his reach now.

With almost his last breath he made a flying leap that brought the figure down to earth.

For a minute or two that seemed to stretch out forever, they struggled there in the snow. Glen fought desperately, frantically, to get away. Jake held him with arms that had suddenly turned to iron.

They rolled closer and closer to the cliff's edge.

Why didn't they come down from the house? Why didn't they see that he had come this way? Wouldn't Helene know that he would come this way? Or did Helene know, and was she purposely keeping silent?

The snow was against his face, in his eyes, blinding him, nearly smothering him.

Let the fool go! He couldn't get far anyway.

Ah, there they came. There were voices in the direction of the house, coming nearer. If only he could hang on another moment or so! Glen heard the voices too, and increased his struggles. Jake felt a sudden blow from Glen's knee that left him gasping for an instant.

Still Jake held on. They clung there to the edge of the cliff, Glen almost over the edge, gasping and struggling, Jake holding him with a frozen grasp. The stones cut against his arms, his face was over the edge, and he could see the gray stones lashed by the black water below. In a moment they would both go over, if help did not come.

Let him go! Much better that way! No—Helene might not

want it. Helene might love the man. Impossible to tell what Helene wanted or didn't want. Hang on to him. Save him for her.
Perhaps Malone could get him an acquittal.

Help was very near now. He could hear them shouting to
him, hear their footsteps.

Just then Glen made one last dying effort. The cliff's edge
began to crumble beneath their weight. In trying to save himself, Jake loosened his grip for just one moment, and in that moment Glen, in his final struggle, wrenched himself free.

Jake saw the twisting, screaming figure plunge down toward
the dark water, strike against a rock that sent him spinning in
another direction, finally collapse on the ice and broken stones
below. For an instant he looked down at the dark, contorted
heap, saw blood beginning to spread over the ice and snow-covered stones. The last, agonized, terrorized scream still rang in
his ears.

Then he felt hands pulling him gently away from the crum-
bling cliffs edge. He looked up and saw Helene's face bending
over him, chalk white. He tried to speak, could not, tried to
move, and felt a sudden blaze of pain. Then everyrthing faded
away, mercifully, into nothing.

He opened his eyes in the Inglehart library. Malone was
bending over him solicitously. He found that he was lying on
the couch, a cover spread over him. His shoulder still pained.

Holly, her face very pale, sat watching him. Helene was
across the room, looking out the window.

"Don't try to move," said Malone, "you dislocated your
shoulder. It's all right now."

He lay quiet for a moment.

"Drink, please." His voice sounded hoarse and strange.

"Sure."

Malone poured brandy down his throat.

He could see Dick's white face, wrinkled with concern.

"Feel better?"

"Much."

"Strong enough to do some listening?" Andy Ahearn asked. "Malone has some explaining to do. But he's been saving it for you."

"Thanks."

Holly spoke up suddenly. "Why did he do it? *Why?*"

Helene continued to stare out the window.

"Because," said Malone gently, "he knew the game was up. You see, my dear, Glen was not your brother, nor was he Alexandria Inglehart's nephew."

"You said that before. But—"

"You were one of twins," said Malone. "You had a twin brother. Your mother died when you were born and your aunt offered Miller, your father, a considerable sum of money if he would sign away all his rights to you and your brother. She wrote that she was mainly interested in the boy, but that she would take you both. Then, before the final arrangements could be made, your twin died."

"Oh," said Holly, and again, "oh."

"Your father found a fatherless baby who had been born at the same time as you and your brother. The mother was glad enough to have her child brought up in luxury. That boy baby was Glen Inglehart."

He paused to mop his face.

"But Nellie Parkins," Jake began, weakly.

"She was Glen's mother," Malone said quietly.

There was a long pause.

"I see it now," Holly said very slowly. "She came here as our nurse. She stayed here to take care of us. She married Parkins and stayed here all these years. And all the time she knew Glen was her child."

Malone nodded.

"Go on," Andy Ahearn said.

"Recently," Malone said, "Miller found himself without money. He came here, told Glen the whole story, produced proof. For a while he was satisfied with blackmailing Glen. Then, realizing that Alexandria Inglehart was an old woman, who didn't have long to live, he decided to get back the agreement he had signed at the time of the twins' birth. With that destroyed, he could claim a share of the estate after her death. Or even better, by going to Alexandria Inglehart herself with the truth, he could blackmail her. With her pride, and her fear of scandal, she would have given him anything rather than have it be known that Glen Inglehart was the illegitimate child of the Inglehart housekeeper. And so Alexandria Inglehart had to die."

"But why Aunt Alex? Why not my father?" Holly asked.

"Because," Malone said, "your father had already reached Alexandria Inglehart with his story. Glen knew it, and Nellie Parkins knew it. Nellie knew that the old woman had sent for her lawyer, to change her will. She planned to cut Glen out of the estate. And Nellie told Glen."

Holly was silent.

"But as luck would have it, Lewis Miller chose that particular night to burglarize the house and get back the agreement. He entered by the window. We can only guess at much of it, but it's near enough. The house was dark. He climbed up on the little roof below the window, looked in, and saw that the old woman was dead. Then he opened the window, which can be done easily from the outside, went in, and rifled the safe, got what he was looking for, and went out again. But while the window can be opened from the outside, it cannot be closed from the outside. I know, because I tried it. So it was left open."

"The safe," Jake said suddenly. "Was it left open, or—"

"I saw it open," Holly said.

Malone nodded. "You did. Miller, in his haste, evidently left it ajar. My guess is that Nellie, who was the first person in the room, saw it, sensed what had happened, and closed it. She'll tell us when she comes to."

"Then Miller kept on blackmailing Glen?" Jake asked. He wished he could have one word with Helene, wished she would stop staring out the window and look at him.

"Probably. But perhaps he felt a certain affection for his daughter. He knew that his evidence might clear her. Yet he didn't want to get himself in trouble with the law. And too, he probably saw a way to make a profit out of what he knew. Lewis Miller was, above all, an opportunist. So he got in touch with Dick Dayton and offered to sell what he knew. Somehow Glen learned that and before Miller had a chance to tell Dayton anything, Glen entered the summerhouse and knocked Dayton unconscious. He didn't kill Miller then, probably because he didn't have an alibi. But he built an alibi for that night, and returned to the summerhouse and murdered him.

"I'm building this," Malone said, "on a flimsy foundation. For according to the theory I had built regarding the method of the crime, only Glen could be guilty. But Glen had absolutely no motive that I could discover. Then there was Miller's phrase to Jake Justus and Helene Brand. '*I am the motive.*' What did it mean? Then when I learned who he was, found that copy of the agreement he had signed, I knew that the motive had something to do with the relationship of Glen, Holly, and Miller. Holly and Glen had been born in St. Louis. That's why I went to St. Louis, looked up old records, and found the motive for the crime. And realized that the striking difference in appearance, character, and everything else between Holly and Glen should have given me a hint at the beginning."

"That tells us why," said Hyme Mendel slowly. "But I still don't see *how*."

"The clocks," said Jake suddenly. "And the beds. And Holly."

"Yes," said Holly, "where *was* I?"

Malone smiled at her.

"You were in bed."

"Do you mean it?"

"I do. You went to bed feeling rather strange, and woke up feeling rather ill. You had been drugged. I guessed that from the beginning, and I think Jake did, too."

Jake nodded. "I did. But I couldn't see any reason."

"The reason was—so that she wouldn't wake when Glen took her out of bed, propped her up in the clothes closet of her room, tied her to the clothes pole to keep her upright, shut the door, and left her there."

"My dream," said Holly slowly. "The coffin standing on end. And darkness. And the rope that kept slipping. And the bruises that were under my arms. But why? What was the reason?"

"It was in case Parkins took it into his head to come into your room. Then while Parkins was getting the car, Glen came and put you back in bed."

"I knew Holly's dream was the key to where she was all the time," said Jake, "but I couldn't unlock anything with it."

"You were trying to unlock the wrong doors," Malone told him.

"But the clocks?"

"All except Parkins' clock were stopped before Glen woke Parkins. Glen's bed, and yours, were made at the same time. When Glen and the Parkinses returned it was easy to slip into your room and make your bed without being seen—make it for the second time that night. Here's the sequence of things.

"Glen stops the clocks, makes his bed and yours, stows you in the closet. Then he wakes Parkins and tells him about the phone call. Parkins dresses and goes to the garage. Glen goes up to his aunt's room—having already killed her, I think—arranges her body so that she will appear to be sitting by the window. Then he puts you back in bed and stops the Parkins' clock."

"And when he came back, with the Parkinses—hours later—he came in and made my bed again?" Holly said.

"That's right."

"But why?"

"Because Glen figured you would react exactly as you did."

"Why?"

"So that you would be arrested for the murder of Alexandria Inglehart."

"Oh!"

"But," said Malone, "while Glen was not actually your brother, he was almost your brother. He had been brought up as your brother. You had played together as children. He wanted you to be accused of the crime, but he didn't want you to suffer for it. So he planned your insanity defense for you." He turned to Ahearn. "When you first heard the story—what did you think?"

"I thought the girl was crazy," Andy Ahearn said.

Jasper Fleck scratched one ear. "It seemed to me like she must of done it, but I was sure she was nuts when she done it."

"I thought the same thing," Malone said, "and any jury

would. Look, Holly. It was probably about three when you woke. Glen knew the drug would run out about that time and he had concealed an alarm clock in his room, right next to yours, to make sure you woke. He knew when you woke, you would be alone in the house with the murdered woman. He wanted to get you up to her room. Hence the clocks.

"When someone wakes up in the night with a stopped clock, what does he do? Frets until he finds out what time it is. Glen knew that you would worry about the time, and about the alarm ringing that had wakened you, and that you would get up and go to his room. You would find him gone, his bed not slept in. You would worry, be upset. Then you would hear a clock ringing in Parkins' room. You would go to the Parkins' room and find them gone, and their bed not slept in. Everywhere you saw a clock, that clock would be stopped at three. And finally, another alarm clock rang, in your Aunt Alex's room. It would take a great deal, he knew, to drive you into that room in the middle of the night, but he estimated that would do it. And it did.

"He knew that you would be weak from the effect of the drug, and that you would be near collapse when you went into that room and found the old woman dead. And you were. He planned everything so that it would look like the working of a disordered mind. That's the reason for the three wounds instead of one—to match the clocks. He planned it so even you would wonder what really did happen that night. And you did. He planned it so that all of us would assume that you had gone mad. And all of us did."

"All but one," said Jake Justus.

She smiled at him gratefully.

"It must have been a blow to him," Malone added, "when he came back and found the window open. That didn't fit. It must have been another blow when Nellie told him about the safe. But he carried out his plans, made your bed before the police came, took the alarm clocks from where he had hidden them and destroyed them, probably threw them into the lake. It must have been more of a blow when you so inexplicably disappeared from jail."

Hyme Mendel had the grace to blush.

"But how," said Andy Ahearn, "how did you find all this out?"

Malone grinned at him. "I didn't. I made it up."

"What the hell?"

Malone nodded. "I've given you a theory, based on certain inescapable facts. You can see how, in view of those facts, the theory cannot help but be correct. Nellie will probably confirm it when she is able to talk.

"The first thing that stuck in my mind was the scarcity of suspects. Holly, Glen, the Parkinses, Miss Brand. Of them, only Holly had a motive. Glen, rather than having any reason for wanting his aunt out of the way, had the best of reasons for wanting her to remain alive—if she was going to disinherit Holly, as we all believed.

"Everything in this case went by threes. The clocks all stopped at three. Three wounds in each murder. Finally, three deaths. And—is it pure coincidence, I wonder—there were three keys that unlocked the truth of what happened.

"The first was Holly's dream. I knew it was important, but I couldn't understand how for a long time. Holly's dream of being hanged, and of being in a coffin standing on end. That, and the narrow clothes closet with the clothes bar, just off her room, hinted that she might have been in the closet during the time she was so mysteriously missing. When she told me tonight that there had been actual bruises where the rope had held her, I knew that theory was correct.

"The second was the telephone. We all assumed that the telephone did ring and that Glen and Parkins both heard it. In fact we assumed that Parkins had probably answered the phone, and called Glen—that would be the normal procedure in the household. No one actually said as much, but it was implied. Implication is much more convincing than fact, as you, Mr. Mendel, being a lawyer, will know. Similarly it was implied so strongly that Parkins knew the old woman was alive when they left the house, that all of us assumed she was alive. When I knew what I had already wondered about, that the telephone could not be heard ringing on the second floor of the house, though Glen claimed he was wakened by its ringing—you see?"

"You said," Jake interrupted, "the only person who could have imitated Holly's voice was Holly herself. But why—"

"What I meant," Malone explained, "was that no one had tried to imitate her voice. Therefore, nobody had telephoned at all." He continued.

"At the very beginning of the case I tried to build a theory on Alexandria Inglehart being dead when Glen and Parkins left the house. But that theory worked only if Glen were the murderer, and I could find no sound motive for Glen murdering his aunt. That was where the third key came into the puzzle and finally unlocked it—Lewis Miller, who *was* the motive for the crime, and died because he was."

There was a longish pause.

"But," said Hyme Mendel uneasily. "The second murder. Why, Glen was here in the room with me. Miller couldn't have been killed before nine o'clock. He was seen in a drugstore in Maple Park at quarter of nine. Glen Inglehart couldn't have murdered him. I was right here with him from nine o'clock till nearly three. Your whole theory falls apart."

"Were you here?"

"Of course I was. He never left the room."

"How do you know what time it was when you got here?"

"I looked at the clock. There's three clocks in the room."

"Not your watch, but at the clocks?"

"Of course. A man doesn't bother to take out his watch when there's three clocks in the room."

"No, he doesn't," said Malone. "Glen knew that. He knew also that when a man looks at a clock—three clocks—and they all say nine o'clock, he doesn't bother to investigate and see if the clock had been set back or not. Glen knew you were coming here because he telephoned and invited you. He had time to get down to the summerhouse and back—Parkins having been gotten out of the house to fix the neighbor's oil burner—and then had time to set back the clocks—"

Jake glanced at Hyme Mendel. He was blushing again.

Jake remembered something. "But Malone. The next day, when we came here—the clocks in this room were stopped—at three."

Malone nodded. "After Hyme here left, Glen set the clocks to three and stopped them again. He wanted us—someone—to find out that the clocks had been stopped deliberately—so that it would be believed Holly had done it."

"But why would she have stopped the clocks? She wouldn't have had any reason to," Hyme Mendel said stupidly. "Why—it would have been insane."

"Exactly," said Malone softly. "You know," he said after a thoughtful pause, "I still think you could have brought her to

trial with the evidence you had and I could have gotten an acquittal on the first ballot with an insanity defense—"

An immediate and furious professional argument followed.

Jake was not interested. He shifted himself painfully and
looked toward the window.

Helene was gone.

CHAPTER 33

"HELL, YOU should kick," said Jake thoughtfully pouring rye into a glass. "You're only starting your honeymoon a few days late."

"Has it only been a few days!" Holly murmured.

"It seems like an eternity," Dick said platitudinously.

"An eternity that I spent in the Blake County jail and at Ma Fraser's."

"Malone works fast," Jake said. "I hate to think what his bill is going to be."

"It's worth it," Holly said, "it's worth anything. Where is Malone, anyway? I haven't seen him since last night, when he told his story."

"Out celebrating," Jake said. "He may not show up for days."

"And Helene?" Dick asked suddenly and tactlessly.

"God knows. I gave up trying to locate her hours ago."

There was an awkward silence.

Jake sighed and poured another drink. "Everything settled. Holly out of jail. Dick recovering from his wounds. The case closed. Dick a hero with a bandage on his bean. Holly a beautiful heiress. Dick and Bride Leave for Honeymoon. World

Wishes Happiness to America's Sweethearts. God, the publicity. Pictures! Whew!"

"You go to hell," Dick said.

"I've posed for pictures till I feel like a Hollywood star," Holly said, "or a baby panda."

"None of my business, but where are you going?"

Dick and Holly looked at each other and laughed.

"We have reservations for Bermuda," Holly said.

"But we're leaving for Grove Falls, Iowa," Dick said, "my home town. My blessed old aunt has forgiven me since all this happened."

"Forgiven you?" Jake asked. "Weren't you speaking?"

"She's a music teacher," Dick told him. "She thinks my band is lousy." He sighed. "For two weeks. Two blessed weeks in a little town. Steve is taking the band. You're managing everything." He suddenly became businesslike. "Keep Steve away from monkey weed if you can. Don't let them play that corny arrangement of *Turkey in the Straw*. I'm leaving you authority to tear up Nelle Brown's contract if she gets a better offer from radio or Hollywood. She's too good for a band singer. But don't hire another canary till I get back. I want one that can sing. You'd probably audition her on a casting couch."

Jake made an unpleasantly rude noise with his lips.

"Two weeks!" Dick said blissfully. He kissed Holly happily.

"Go away," said Jake fretfully. "You make me sick."

Holly looked at him with sudden sympathy. "It is rather a shame. You did most of the work. You took most of the risks. You got everything all straightened out for us and now you're being left behind."

"Don't thank me, thank Malone," Jake said. "Of course, you

could always take me on your honeymoon instead of Dick. I'm not so good-looking, but I'm more fun."

He poured another round of drinks.

"To your happiness and all that stuff."

He poured another.

"To John Joseph Malone."

A third.

"To Ma Fraser."

"Yes," said Holly, "and what am I going to do with the two dozen hand-embroidered dish towels that she gave me for a wedding present—with hand-crocheted edges that she made herself—living in hotel rooms with a traveling band leader?"

"Don't worry," said Dick, "I'll buy you a dish to wash some day. What am *I* going to do with the live lamb the orchestra boys gave us for a wedding present? The manager says we can't keep it in the hotel basement any longer."

"I'll fix that," Jake promised. "I'll give it to Malone for his fee."

Holly poured the fourth drink.

"To you, Jake."

"Thank you."

They told him good-by and went away. He sighed deeply and looked around his hotel room. It was suddenly a dreary place. Nothing to do. Everything all settled. No more frantic driving around Chicago with an escaped murder suspect wrapped up in bandages. No more wild ideas to carry out. No more fights on the edges of cliffs. Nothing to do but keep an eye on the damn band and see to its publicity and keep Steve out of jail and Nelle Brown out of the papers. Nothing to do but get drunk.

He opened the new bottle of rye.

There was a timid knock on the door.

"Come in!"

The door opened slowly. There stood Helene, as he had seen her for the first time, fur coat, blue satin pajamas, galoshes. And drunk as a camel.

He hauled her through the door and shoved her into a chair. "Where the hell did you go?"

She sighed and shook her head. "Give me a drink, Jake."

He handed it to her and repeated his question.

She turned her face away from him. "I just sort of wanted to be away somewhere, if you know what I mean."

"I think I have a rough idea."

"I mean after all, when a girl's known a guy all her life, and she's sort of considered marrying him, and all of a sudden he turns out to be a murderer and falls off the edge of a cliff, it's sort of surprising anyway."

"Sure," said Jake sympathetically, kneeling by the chair and putting his arms around her very gently.

"So I just went home and put on my pajamas to settle down and think about it, and then I got restless, so I got the car out and I've been driving around."

"Ever since?"

"Yes."

"And you're still alive!" He regarded her admiringly.

"What's happened to that guy Malone? I need him."

"He's probably out on a bender," Jake said. "It's the close of a case. Why?"

"I've got more damned tickets. Speeding, reckless driving, every other thing. I'll be in jail for life."

"You sure as hell do need a lawyer," Jake told her, "on a permanent basis. I think you need a manager, too." He looked at her meditatively.

Conversation lagged for the space of two drinks apiece.

"You know," said Jake suddenly, "I tried to save him."

Pause.

"I know you did," said Helene. "I'm glad you didn't. It was better the way it happened. Quicker. Cleaner."

Longer pause.

Jake moved to the arm of her chair.

"Well," he said thoughtfully, "it's like this. We've found the murderer, the case is closed, Holly is out of trouble, she and Dick have left for their honeymoon, as far as I know the band is doing all right, and it looks as though we might have an evening to ourselves. Can you think of any possible interruptions?"

She shook her head.

He took the glass from her hand, set it on the dresser, extinguished his cigarette.

"In that case—" said Jake Justus.

For the second time he noticed how those blue satin pajamas seemed to grow warm under his touch. Helene lifted her face to his.

At that instant there was a sudden, thundering knocking at the door.

They looked at each other for a moment, then Jake opened the door to admit John J. Malone, his tie under his ear, a bottle under each arm.

"Fate!" said Jake to Helene. "This is the end!"

THE END

DISCUSSION QUESTIONS

- What kind of detective is John J. Malone? How does he compare to other series sleuths you have encountered?

- Were you able to predict any part of the solution to the case?

- After learning the solution, were there any clues you realized you had missed?

- Would the story be different if it were set in the present day? If so, how?

- Did the social context of the time play a role in the narrative? If so, how?

- What role did the Chicago setting play in the narrative? Would the story have been different if it were set someplace else?

- If you were one of the main characters, would you have acted differently at any point in the story?

- Did you identify with any of the characters? If so, which?

- Did *Eight Faces at Three* remind you of any other books you've read?